The Last Warner woman

Also by Kei Miller

The Same Earth

The Last Warner Woman

KEI MILLER

Weidenfeld & Nicolson
LONDON

First published in Great Britain in 2010
by Weidenfeld & Nicolson
An imprint of the Orion Publishing Group Ltd
Orion House, 5 Upper St Martin's Lane
London WC2H 9EA

An Hachette UK Company

1 3 5 7 9 10 8 6 4 2

A CIP catalogue record of this book is
available from the British Library

ISBN 978 0 297 86079 2 (trade paperback)
ISBN 978 0 297 86077 8 (cased)

'The Warner Woman' by Edward Baugh reproduced
with permission of Sandberry Press, Toronto, Canada.
'Hurricane Hits England' by Grace Nichols reproduced
with permission of the Curtis Brown Group.

This is a work of fiction. Names, characters, places and incidents
are either the product of the author's imagination or are
used fictitiously.

Typeset by Input Data Services Ltd, Bridgwater, Somerset

Printed and bound in Great Britain by Clays Ltd, St Ives plc

The Orion Publishing Group's policy is to use papers that
are natural, renewable and recyclable products and
made from wood grown in sustainable forests. The logging
and manufacturing processes are expected to conform to
the environmental regulations of the country of origin.

www.orionbooks.co.uk

The blue sky broke. The warner-woman.
Bell-mouthed and biblical
she trumpeted out of the hills
prophet of doom, prophet of God,
breeze-blow and earthquake,
tidal wave and flood.

I crouched, I cowered, I remembered Port Royal.
I could see the waters of East Harbour rise.
I saw them heave Caneside bridge. Dear God,
don't make me die, not now, not yet.

Well, the sky regained its blue composure.
Day wound slowly down to darkness.
Lunch-time came, then supper-time,
then dream-time and forgetting.
Haven't heard a warner-woman
these thirty-odd years.

The Warner Woman, Edward Baugh

Talk to me Huracan
Talk to me Oya
Talk to me Shango
And Hattie,
My sweeping, back-home cousin.

Tell me why you visit
An English coast?
What is the meaning
Of old tongues
Reaping havoc
In new places?

Hurricane Hits England, Grace Nichols

HOW THE STORY WILL UNFOLD

Part One

in which the story begins

Part Two

in which the story prepares to travel,
and then begins again

Part Three

in which others bear witness
to the story

Part Four

in which the story invents
parables, and speaks a benediction
and then ends

Part One

IN WHICH THE STORY BEGINS

The Purple Doily

Once upon a time there was a leper colony in Jamaica. If you wanted to get there today, you would have to find a man by the name of Ernie McIntyre but who you would simply call Mr Mac, at his own insistence and also the insistence of others, including his own mother, who knew him by no other name. Mr Mac was famous for his great big belly, so surprisingly big that the buttons on the one side of his shirt were permanently estranged from the holes they were supposed to be married to on the other; he also had a great big head, and a sprawling set of buttocks, all of which he could somehow manage to squeeze in to the front seat of his Lada taxi, you in the passenger seat, and then make the wild jerky ascent up the red dirt road lined on each side with the broad green leaves of banana trees. When the car reached the crest of the hill, Mr Mac would stop — a welcome break, because if no one had warned you before about Mr Mac's driving, how he would press on the gas from the bottom of the hill and never ease off, not for any corner, not for any dip, not for any rock in the middle of the road, just gas gas gas all the way up, the whole time giving you his own tour guide speech in a strange language which, even if you could understand it, you would not hear because of the diesel engine; and if no one had warned you about all of this and you had made the great mistake of having a full breakfast, then all of that food would have churned up and you would now be feeling close to sick.

3

On the crest of the hill you would tumble out of the taxi, holding your stomach, while Mr Mac excitedly pointed to something below.

'Look, mate.'

He would say this word, mate, because maybe you are from England and he is trying to impress you, but thereafter his speech would be lost to you.

'Dung deh suh it deh. Yu nuh see it? Dung deh suh! Look nuh! Den wha mek yu a hole on pon yu belly like seh birt pain a hit yu? Look. See de zinc roof dem pint up through de mist. Deh suh we a guh.'

You would not understand Mr Mac completely, but you would look to where he was pointing and some of the words would then come together to make a kind of sense, for indeed, down there in the valley, there were zinc roofs pointing up through the mist. And that's where you were going. Just as the Original Pearline Portious had back in 1941 while her mother stood frozen under a guava tree. Pearline had stood on this same crest of hilltop, except she had arrived by her own two feet. She had also looked down on the zinc roofs and made the decision to walk down to them. This despite her seventeen years of living in these mountains and never before having set foot on the trail. If she had continued to listen to the wise counsel of her family and friends and all those who lived in the mountains, she would not have made this journey, for they had said over and over that down there in the valley was a place of terrible sickness.

But it wasn't curiosity that led Pearline Portious down the trail, unwittingly changing her life: that day she needed to sell a purple doily.

The colour purple was a strange choice for a doily. It was accepted wisdom on the island that anything designed to cover wooden surfaces – tablecloths, crocheted mats or doilies – was supposed to be white. Pearline's determination to crochet and knit in colour – pink, blue, red, green, purple – meant that not a single one of her

4

creations had ever been sold. The absolute failure of what was supposed to be an entrepreneurial endeavour did not upset Pearline. She considered herself an artist, and of the kind whose chief aim was to please herself. Every unsold item would then truly belong to her and she took great pleasure in finding a place for them in her room. It was a room which everyone in the village had toured and reluctantly admitted, despite being convinced that each individual item was ugly, that the combination was something wonderful. They said it was as if the child lived inside a rainbow.

Pearline's mother, of course, tried desperately to dissuade her daughter from her useless and colourful habits. That very morning she had observed her daughter knitting the purple doily under a guava tree.

'Pearline girl, look on what you is doing nuh! It is just ugly. Nobody is going to buy something like that. You cannot afford to always be making things for yu own self.'

'Mama. I will get this one sold. I promise.'

'Eh! You can't even look me in the eyes and say that. Girl, you is just wasting yu time. Who going to buy that from you? We even looking on the same thing? It is purple, girl. *Purple*. Who you ever see with a purple doily in them good, good house?'

'I say I will get it sold, Mama.'

'Saying you going to get it sold not going to get it sold, Pearline. You is only full of talk. Look at me, girl. Is high time you grow up. And don't puff up yu face at me neither. I saying these things for yu own good. Me and yu father giving you money dat we never just pick up out-a road. And we giving it to you only for you to make these ... these purple pieces of stupidness that not going a damn place except inside yu room.'

Pearline's ten fingers began to tremble. They became useless, unable to continue the knitting that had happily occupied them moments before. She kept her eyes fixed to the ground, not wanting to look up. Her mother was also trembling in anger. She had not intended this confrontation to become so big a thing, and yet she knew it had to become bigger still. Having embarked on this road, she had to walk its full length. So she stepped out of her slippers and on to the earth so her daughter would understand that the next words out of her mouth were serious.

'All right, girl. All right. You say you is going to sell this one? Well fine. Go and sell it. And I swear to you I will stay here on this piece of ground until that happen. Come thunderstorm or sunhot, I not moving. You hear me, child? Jesus Son of Mary would have to come down off him cross to move me. Cause is like you take me for some kind of poppyshow.'

Pearline finally looked up, astonished. She knew that this threat was real, for mothers were always doing things like that. Her mama would stay right there. She would not go inside to sit or to cook or to sleep. She would not go to the farm ground to work. She would make the neighbours pass and see her as rooted as the tree she was standing under, and she would explain to them that it was her daughter who had made her into a poppyshow. She would stay there, even for days, until Pearline had either sold the doily or come back to apologise saying *Mama, you were right. It is time I grow up.*

So the Original Pearline Portious went off to the market, desperate to do what she had never been able to do before.

The market on a Saturday morning is always a brand-new city that rises, as if by magic, with the sun. Its newness, however, does not make it clean. It is a hot, stinking place full of that special breed of fly that remains unimpressed by the hands that constantly swat at it. The city's lanes overflow with chocho, pumpkin, gungo peas, green bunches of callaloo and pods of yellow ackee. Women shout from their various stalls, their foreheads glistening under their bandanas: *Yam! Dasheen! Cocoa!* – each one holding out a scale, weighing a pound of this or a half-pound of that, always careful to give a little extra so that customers, convinced they had secured a bargain, would come back. The fish-women gather around concrete sinks and run metal files up and down the bodies of snappers and mackerel; bright silver scales jump into the air and land softly on the women's heads like confetti. They call out, *Snapper! Sprat! Goatfish!* And an Indian man standing by a cart of cane, a sharp cutlass in his hand, sings out *Sweet sugar cane!* – though he isn't quite as musical as the tall gentleman, his head wrapped in a turban, who walks up and down the lanes singing his one long note, *Brooomie, brooomie,* a faggot of brooms stretched across his shoulders like he was in the middle of his own crucifixion.

It was amid such a cacophony that the Original Pearline Portious tried to advertise her purple doily. *Pretty doily for sale! Pretty doily for sale!* She pleaded and she jostled and she pushed it into people's faces. *Ma'am, just take a look nuh. Look how it would look nice in yu house. Pretty doily for sale.*

But no one paid her the slightest mind.

The market on a Saturday afternoon is always a quieter place than in the morning. The crowds have thinned. The lanes no longer overflow with produce. The ice from the fish stalls has melted and even the annoying flies, finished with their own shopping, it would seem, have taken off. The vendors are more relaxed and throw their words easily at one another instead of at the customers. The best of their goods will have gone, and even they have a kind of pity for stragglers who are only now coming to shop and have to search through the best of their blighted goods.

But on the Saturday in question, there was one young woman still trying to make her first and only sale. *Pretty doily for sale! Pretty doily for sale! Please ma'am, sir, just take a look nuh. Look how it would look nice in yu house. Pretty doily for sale. I selling it cheap, cheap.*

Still no customer paid her the slightest mind and it was instead the somewhat infamous shoe vendor, Maizy, who finally took notice.

Like many Jamaican market women, Maizy was a creature for whom derision was an art. So committed was she to this practice that there were days when she counted it a greater success to have landed the most insults than to have sold any pairs of shoes. To Pearline's great misfortune it was this Maizy who now took notice of her, and of the ugly doily that swung dejectedly from her fingers.

Maizy nudged her neighbour, Flo. With a pout of her lips she pointed out the pathetic figure of Pearline. Flo grinned.

'Darling, is the same doily you have there selling from this morning, or is a wholeheap of them that you did bring? Please tell me is a wholeheap you did bring!'

'But Flo' declared Maizy on cue, 'you is a wicked, wicked woman to wish this child did make wholeheap *more* of that thing she have there selling. I can't even call it a doily. You have no idea the damage that thing can do?'

'What you saying to me, Maizy?'

'Mi dear! It is sake of a purple something look just like that that cause my neighbour hog to drop down dead last week.'

'No!'

'Flo, God's truth! If I lie, I die! My poor neighbour, Miss Esmi – the same one with the twist-up mouth – well, she come home last week and find a purple doily just like that one, fling down pon her table.'

'But how something like that get there?'

'Must be her husband, missis! You know he blind from morning. Well must be him did buy it and put it down there fi her. Or else somebody was trying to work obeah against her. Well anyhow, Miss Esmi was so frighten when she see it there, she just pawn it up and dash it out the window. And that is how her hog get it and try fi eat it. Mi dear, as to how Miss Esmi tell it, the hog barely take one bite and, just suh, it collapse, keel over and dead! Imagine that, the hog dead from purple.'

'Lawd-have-mercy-sweet-Jesus, Maizy! You mean to tell me this girl here is selling a powerful Hog-Killer?'

'That is what I telling you, Flo. If she make any more all the hog in Jamaica bound to be dead by next week.'

Duly satisfied with their own wickedness, Maizy and Flo held their equatorial bellies, slapped their thighs and began to laugh. Between gulps of breath, Maizy managed to turn to Pearline and say, 'Mi dear girl child, I think is best you try your hand at something else, because ...' she started laughing and hiccuping again, 'it don't look like sewing is fi you at all, at all.'

Pearline slouched and dragged her feet away from the two laughing women. But she continued to call out, with even less conviction now, Pretty doily for sale. Doily for sale.

✷

The market on a Saturday night was a lonely place. The crowds had vanished and the blue tarpaulin that had once been like a sky stretched over the lanes had been taken down and folded up. By then, the vendors had exchanged their mangoes and sweetsops and melons and whatever it was they could not bother to take back home, and one by one, they climbed aboard rickety buses and departed. Pearline alone remained, the salt wind from the sea whistling through the now empty stalls. A dog with pronounced ribs walked around the market sniffing out morsels of food. He approached Pearline and eyed her with suspicion. Pretty doily for sale, she pleaded. But even he turned up his nose and walked away.

And so it was Pearline had come to the end of her childhood. Her mother was right; she had really believed that just saying she would get the doily sold would have got it sold. She thought it had been her attachment to the items that had shielded them

9

from the desire of customers, but now she was forced to face the truth: not that her creations were ugly, but that the world was not a thing to have faith in. She understood it now for the blind, deaf and uncaring thing it was. For had she not called out to it for a whole day, called until her voice was gone, and the world had not heard her. And had she not shoved the purple doily into the world's eyes, but the world had not seen it. So it was with these thoughts that Pearline did exactly what her mother had wanted her to do: she grew up.

But maybe she was not ready for so sudden a growth. The poor girl's mind short-circuited, shut itself down, and when she finally left the market she was in a deep trance. Her walk was a peculiar one, catatonic, and it led her down roads she had never been on before. She was like a ghost haunting the island, her head tilted to one side, her mind to another, and her feet simply following the road, marching in the direction of darkness which is, of course, no direction at all.

She passed several hours like this. Dogs barked at her. Thieves avoided her. And then the sky, which had mostly been a deep navy blue, turned black, and then just as suddenly the darkness began to fade. It became silver with pink edges. Roosters began to crow, and this is where it happened, the Original Pearline Portious found herself standing on the same crest of a hill to which, in later years, Mr Mac might take you. She looked down on the zinc roofs pointing up through the mist and made the decision. Despite what everyone had told her, she took the trail down towards the terrible place of sickness, a place she had never been to before.

✳

The leper colony sat quietly and undisturbed in a valley between the Stone Hill mountains of St Catherine. It was surrounded by a mile of green chain-link fence, ten feet high, which was supposed to be there for security. In another colony in another part of the world, thirty-two patients had crept up to their guards one night and in the ensuing battle of sores and nails and teeth and batons and limbs and guns, ten patients were killed, four wounded and one guard infected. When news of this episode spread, leprosariums all over the world began to build fences. The one which surrounded St Catherine, however, was pointless. The fence was not topped by barbed wire; there was no guard patrolling its length; there were several trees which grew right beside it; but most significantly, there was a gate and it was always kept open.

In the history of the leper colony no one had ever tried to get out, and before Pearline Portious in 1941, no one had tried to get in.

The three zinc roofs belonged to three wooden bungalows. They faced away from the gate, so that when Pearline arrived all she could see were three broad wooden backsides turned dismissively towards her. But a man was kneeling in the dirt before her, muttering as his blue-veined hands slapped broken eggshells into the soil. Pearline walked over and her shadow fell on him.

'Yes, Miss Lazarus, what now?' the man snapped without looking up.

His voice was old. Pearline would find out later that his name was Albert Dennis and that he was unfriendly to almost everyone. But no one received the brunt of his bad temper more than Agatha Lazarus. The woman frequently snuck up on him like this, making herself known only as a shadow across his gardening, or a combination of smells he had come to despise: oranges she had just squeezed, lemon-grass tea she had just brewed, and talcum powder she had just patted on to her breasts to keep them cool. So when the present shadow did not make a sound – no request for eggs, milk, bottles of disinfectant, bandages – Albert looked up and found instead the Original Pearline Portious, shivering.

Now Pearline's mother had been quite serious. She was going to stay under that guava tree come rain or sunhot. But before such forces could arrive and test her resolve – indeed, within just an hour – a more pressing matter from within her own body had presented itself. It was 9.30 in the morning. She had eaten a rather heavy breakfast one and a half hours earlier. Now, like clockwork, she needed, badly, desperately, to shit.

Her sphincter muscles contracted in and out; she tried to fan herself; she sang a hymn; she farted loudly and pungently. *Oh Lawd, Oh Lawd,* she thought, until finally she shouted to her husband inside.

'Devon! Devonooooohhhh! Grab de chimmy pot from underneat de bed! Mek haste!'

Devon appeared in the doorway of the small house and stopped to scratch his dark balding head. He was confused. He considered the form of his wife, muttering and fanning herself under the tree. He was going to ask her sternly, *Dorcas, why in God's green earth you want the chimmy pot? You is really going to doodoo out there, in the broad and living daylight, for the entire world to see?* But one look at her face, the mixture of anger and strain contorting it, made him swallow his questions and scamper inside.

This then, was the surest testament of a mother's love for her one daughter – that in the broad and living daylight she had shat under a guava tree, her only privacy the floral skirt she was wearing that fanned out covering her lower parts and the chimmy pot she was stooped over.

✼

What a conundrum of colours Pearline had suddenly found herself in: she was afraid because the man kneeling before her was white;

she was afraid because now that he was looking up at her, with even more annoyance in his eyes than there had been in his voice, she saw that those eyes were blue; she was afraid because she had been walking all night and her own eyes were surely red and she was suddenly conscious of her whole dishevelled appearance; she was afraid because the doily in her hand was purple and she wondered whether this would offend the man as it had apparently offended everyone else. She wished now that the doily was white so she could hold it out to him like a flag of peace.

'I never mean to disturb you, Mister Man Sir. I have this doily here selling. I was just wondering if I could interest you in it. I am ...' and the words stuck. Pearline began to doubt herself. But finally she finished the sentence, ' ... I am very good at knitting, sir.'

Albert Dennis got to his feet, taking hold of the purple doily in his slow climb towards the sky. His lean height now made her feel small and instead of looking down on his stooped figure, she now had to shield her face from the sun. Pearline was familiar with men of the clergy – deacons, reverends, pastors, parsons and lay preachers. They were part of her village, and she had seen them during the week in their dirty water-boots just like everyone else. She had also seen them on Sundays, freshly scrubbed and wearing their one good suit. But Pearline Portious had never before seen a priest, though they had been described to her in detail: *mi dear, dem wear a big ugly frock just like woman, and one something on top them head that you can't even call a proper hat, and to hear them on Sunday is like torture, for is a long-drawn-out sermon in Latin or what-have-you because that is how high-standing people believe the Saviour himself talk.*

Albert Dennis was not in a frock or a strange hat but Pearline still knew he was a priest because of another distinguishing feature that had been described – a large wooden cross dangling from their necks, and on that cross a tiny crucified Christ.

Monsignor Dennis kept his eyes on Pearline but his fingers were

13

inspecting her work, pulling the doily, feeling its surface. She awaited his verdict.

'My dear young lady,' he said finally, 'you indeed are very good at knitting. I believe the Lord might have sent you to us.'

'Oh yes, sir. Oh yes. The Lord him own self call me down here today.'

She suddenly imagined an abundance of furniture filling the three bungalows – nightstands, coffee tables, dinner tables, desks, bureaus, whatnots, chest-of-drawers, dressers, cabinets, shelves; all of them wooden and bare, just waiting for her knitted creations to cover them.

'I was saying my morning prayers in bed this morning, sir, and I hear when God say to me, Pearline girl, mek haste and go down to the valley today today. They need a girl like you.'

'Very well ...'

'Yes sir. I can do mats too, tablecloths, doilies, blankets, even clothes like sweater and all them things there, and even ...'

'Then, my dear,' the priest interrupted her sharply, 'you will be able to knit something much simpler.'

'Sir?'

'Just a band, my dear, about this wide.' With his thumb and index finger, he indicated the width of about three inches.

'And this tall.' He indicated the length from the ground to his waist. 'And it must be white.'

Pearline's excitement vanished. 'Ongly that, sir?'

'Only that.'

'Ongly that. One so-so ...' She didn't even know what to name this thing she was being asked to make. 'One so-so ... something that is this wide and this tall?'

'Not just one. As many as you are able to make.'

'But ongly that, sir?'

It was the simplicity of the request that was disappointing, a mere twenty-four stitches across, chaining and turning, chaining

14

and turning, row after row until she reached the required four feet.

'Only that, young lady. Come back next week about this time with what you've done and I will buy them from you. Now, good morning.'

The priest bowed his head politely and Pearline understood she had been dismissed. She turned to leave but then remembered her mother.

'Beg pardon, sir, but the doily you have there is not free.'

He looked down at his hands and gave a slight start having quite forgotten what he was holding. Indeed, he hadn't intended on purchasing a thing so ... so purple, but he fished in his pockets nonetheless and deposited thirty cents into Pearline Portious's proffered hands. This was, of course, once upon a time when thirty cents was worth more than it is now.

Arriving back at the yard which she had left the day before, Pearline Portious found that her mother was still underneath the guava tree. She had fallen asleep in the dirt, her head resting on the pillow of her clasped hands. Pearline carefully placed the three ten-cent coins on her mother's cheek and watched as her eyes fluttered open at the cold feel of metal on her face.

'See there!' Pearline hissed triumphantly, towering over the confused woman. 'I tell you I would get the doily sold.'

Two teardrops sprang up from her mother's eyes. They rolled horizontally to meet the coins, and Pearline's arrogance vanished. She understood now why she had been successful: it was her mother's prayer – a desperation which had gone out into the world to accomplish what had never been accomplished before. She sat down while her mother lifted herself to a sitting position.

'You really get it sold, child?'

'Yes, Mama ... but you was right too. It is time I grow up.'

an instalment of a testimony spoken to the wind

Shhhhhhhhh

I DON'T KNOW who you is. I don't know where in the world you even is right now, but I believe you is there, sitting down, comfortable as you please, and that you is hearing me. I need to talk what I talking soft. I must not wake up the samfie man who I discover is writing down all manner of lies for you. He is writing down my story as if that story was a snake — the snake from the garden — twisting, coiling, bending this way and that. But hear me now, if his words is a snake, then mine is a mongoose chasing after him, a terror of teeth that him will be scared of. I going to set the record right. I going to unbend the truth. So listen close.

Shhhhhhhhh

That sound is the wind, and this is what I going to write my story on. I was made to understand this from I was just a girl — be careful what you talk, Mother Lazarus used to tell me, careful or else the four winds will take it up like a kite that loss its owner, take it far, far to those whose ears you never want to hear it. But I don't care who hear me tonight. I ongly care that somebody does. So I standing up on this little piece of balcony like how the queen sometimes stand in front of her palace. I standing up in this terrible cold without a shawl or a coat to brace me. I standing up in this country where I have come to till a hard ground. It so dark I cannot even see the snow falling, but when I open my mouth the snowflakes fall like dots on my tongue. Like little fullstops. As if even

18

the snow is trying to say, *end your talk now, lady, and don't say those things you is bout to say*. But it has always been like this. Whenever I did get a word or a prophecy, whenever I did feel the spirit jump on me, whenever I did feel the crossroad drawing me to its pulpit, begging me to stand in the middle-road and say on to all who did have ears to hear, *Consider the words of the Lord* ... well, those times it was like the whole world want to close its ears and its eyes and its doors. The sons and daughters of earth always trying to run away from warning. But understand me now, I going to stand up and talk same way whether your heart is stone or it is feather, and whether this snow tell me to stop or to go on. I going to stand here every night and talk my testimony. I ongly hope that the wind will take it up, and that you is somewhere in the world listening, cause if you read what I did read, that Once Upon A Time There Was A Leper Colony In Jamaica, then you need to understand something straight away: that is a make-up story, a lie from the pit of hell.

Shhhhhhhhh

It wasn't once upon a time. It is still there today and I can go back and visit any time I wants to. If my mind take me and I decide to finally leave this godforsaken country and go back mongst my own people, I could do it, and all of it would be there: the veranda, the rocking chairs, the smell of Dettol. There is no evidence to say that such a time was once and no more. And something else you should know: it wasn't no colony. It was just a simple house. A hospice is the word they did call it. It was on Queen Margaret Drive, number 35, in Spanish Town. You heard me right: Spanish Town. Not no valley between

19

Stone Hill mountains. Not no deep back-a-God country part of the island with cow and callaloo and yam. Just the ugly squalor of Spanish Town – same place the news today say is full of gunshot and gullies. Full of galvan houses squashed on top of each other. Full of poor people who have to live their lives in fear, because the city just too full of tief and liard and murderers. I used to give warnings to that city. I warn till I was tired. I would go down near the market and stand up mongst all the buses and say what the Spirit did lay on my heart to say. Even the prisoners up there, high above the cricket ground in them cages, would listen. Most days they used to make fun by calling out to people below: *Hey you! Yes, you! I see you and I mark you, and when time I get out I going to massacre you every which way!* They was ongly teasing people, but people would still get fraid for true. And if you was a woman they would tell you bout your woman-parts, and how much man did breed you already, and all manner of slackness. But when they see me, not a word. They quiet down and listen to whatever it is I had to say. One time I even hear a terrible cowbawling, like it was coming from the sky. It was one of those boys up in that prison, like he find out that day that he wasn't badder than God. Like God break his heart and make it soft, and he catch the spirit from my words. He was up there in the towers bawling JEESUS, JEESUS FORGIVE ME, like he know that the earthquake I was calling for would rock him even up there and rock him straight into hell. I warn that city like how Jonah did warn Nineveh, and like how the angels did warn Gomorrah.

Shhhhhhhhh

But you need to know something about Jamaica. There was a time when prophecies did take root, but another time when the same prophecies turn to dust. One day the government and the CIA start to hand out guns instead of flour or rice. People realise they was hungry for something else. We was a people who did beat down too long, and the guns make some of we feel mighty. First we use the guns to kill each other, then we use the guns to kill our own country, and we would have used them to kill God if God could be killed. We wasn't afraid of nothing no more, and the wickedness start to rise. That is the Spanish Town that I grow up in, and where the lepers did live.

Shhhhhhhhh

I grow up in that house on Queen Margaret Drive and in truth it was a better street than most. Every house was painted a soft colour – blue or green or pink. Maybe people did live a hard life and they wanted to look on to their houses and see something soft. Number 35 used to be pink, but when I was growing up the paint did start to peel and the latticework did start to fall down. This lattice wasn't just decoration. It was put up round the house so that nobody from the road could see on to the veranda. People was mighty inquisitive and would always fast into things they had no business fasting into. The lattice was there so that no biblewoman passing, or no postman dropping off letters, or no pickney walking home from school, could just look and see the kind of people that did sit on that veranda every day, in their rocking chairs, with feet ugly and swollen beyond the possibility of shoes. It is plenty years now that I don't think of these

21

people, but once upon a time they was my only family. Maas Paul and Miss Lily, and Maas Johnson and Maas Johnny. And of course there was Mother Lazarus.

Shhhhhhhhh

But look at how I forget my manners. I talking up a storm and I don't introduce myself. Well the name you can call me is Ada, which is short for Adamine, and that is my true, true name. It is the name my mother did intend for me to have, and what everyone call me when I was growing up. But since then I find out that this name is not on my birth paper. The name written down there was Pearline Portious, and I figure this would make me, not the Original, but Pearline Portious the Second.

Shhhhhhhhh

I tell you what though — when Mr Writer Man did start to write this story, he should have put down two words to begin it all. Crick, Crack. And if he did start the story like that we would all know that his world was just make-believe. We would know his world was the world of Brer Anansi and Brer Tiger and the magic-pot and what-have-you. If I was to start my true true story, I would start it like this

My name is Adamine Bustamante, and I did born amongst the lepers.

A Colony of Colours

Perhaps it was the man's whiteness, for in those days which black girl would dare question a man of such pedigree? How else to explain the utter lack of curiosity that infected the Original Pearline Portious? For six months she, who lived in a rainbow room, slipped into a life as monotonous and dull as the 'ongly thats' she had begun to knit. She was making them in great abundance. Every Saturday she would scrape them into a plastic bag and make her way back down to the colony, along the path that smelt always of wet grass and mangoes. She would step through the open gate where Monsignor Dennis seemed always to be waiting on her. She would give him the bag of knitting and he in turn would give her money. This exchange was not even accompanied by words – no howdy-do, no good-afternoon, no see-you-same-time-next-week, and certainly no questions from Pearline about *what kind of place is this? What is it that goes on here?*

And it wasn't that the leper colony had been nothing but silence. There were occasional sounds from inside the bungalows – coughs, low voices, the scraping of chairs, and other little things that should have confirmed to Pearline that the place was being lived in and used. But she was not curious about such things, and did not realise it was the priest himself who stopped her questions. His face and his manner had become a kind of wall, and so while Pearline did hear evidence of other lives being lived behind the priest, she never thought to ask about them.

Also, during those six months, her departure from the colony was always attended by the smell of oranges, lemon-grass and talcum powder. But she got used to this too and it simply became, for her, the scent of leaving.

Then one day Monsignor Dennis said a strange thing.

'My dear young lady, I am going away for a while. You must not come back here for a few weeks. Do you understand?' His voice often did this – said soft things like 'dear lady' yet remained hard. 'You are to stay away from here. For a month at least. When I come back I will buy everything you have made in the meantime. Do you understand?'

In fact, she understood him more than he wanted to be understood. The priest's words had become the wall his face and his demeanour had been before. And because the wall was no longer amorphous, because it was now fully formed and articulated, Pearline could see it, and because she could see it, she at last tried to look over it.

'Sir?'

'Yes, my dear?'

'Sir, I fraid I don't understand you too well. Explain again.'

Albert Dennis raised his eyebrows, and then said slowly but sharply, 'There is nothing difficult in my instructions, young lady. If you don't understand, it is because you are choosing not to. Now listen, I am going away for a month ...'

'But there is other people here, sir,' Pearline cut in. 'I can't tell you who them be or what them look like. I never lay eyes on them. But I don't understand why you can't get one of them to take these things next Saturday?'

'You impertinent girl! It cannot be done!'

Pearline observed the veins on the priest's neck bunched together like an angry chicken; she observed his trembling lips and she realised how angry she had made him. She was about to ask pardon for her rudeness but then something flickered. She looked up to

24

see, for the first time in that valley, standing right behind the priest, another human being.

'But yes indeedy, Missa Dennis,' the newcomer said, 'it can be done.'

Monsignor Dennis's face creased into another kind of annoyance, an older one that his face seemed to settle into without much effort.

'Miss Lazarus, what the devil is it now?' he said as he turned around.

The woman looked on Monsignor Dennis as a mother might look on a child who has thrown a tantrum. She wore a broad red calico skirt and two shirts – the first buttoned all the way up and the second unbuttoned, but tied under her bosoms so that each half cupped one of her magnificent breasts. She was a small woman with steel-grey hair that grew tall and wide like the top of a tree. You could tell she was old because of her feet, and because of the wrinkles as fine as scripture that spread out like sunbeams from around her eyes. The eyes themselves could fool you though, for they were as brown and bright as a baby's.

She stepped past the priest, ignoring his question, and reached for Pearline's hands.

'Call me Mother Lazarus, child. You must come back here next Saturday, same as always. Because who to tell, Missa Dennis might be gone much longer than even he think he supposed to be gone for.'

'I forbid it.' Monsignor Dennis protested, but he said the words without conviction.

Mother Lazarus, still holding on to Pearline's hands, said simply, 'It is time.'

❈

Agatha Lazarus's problem was that her every step and smile and laugh and wink was filled with so much energy, so much warmth, that no one ever considered the simple fact that became more true with each passing year: she was old. So it wasn't bad-mindedness, nor spitefulness, nor lack of regard that made people not notice her stooped back, her steel-grey hair, or her wrinkled face. It was simply that around Agatha, sadness had a way of dissipating and lethargy a way of vanishing. And around her, newly energised, people thought that this energy was her own. And in a way it was. It was her gift to them, but it was a gift that did not take up residence in her own bones. Agatha alone felt her arthritis going deeper and deeper. She alone saw her days dwindling. She alone knew it would soon be time to retire, not just from her day-to-day job, but from life. When she said as much to Monsignor Dennis he would listen without sympathy. He was sixty-five years old and still could not imagine that Agatha Lazarus was over twenty years his senior.

On the morning that the Original Pearline Portious had made her first descent to the leper colony, Mother Lazarus had also made her own very painful and lumbering descent on to her knees where she prayed. She did not believe in God, but she believed in Desperation. She believed Desperation could make a woman go down on her knees, and that that same Desperation would go out into the world in search of whatever was needed. Mother Lazarus was desperate for a replacement, a young woman brave enough to enter a leper colony, to touch the inhabitants without flinching, to wash floors, cook food and bandage wounds.

When she had looked outside that morning and seen Pearline talking, excitedly it seemed, to Monsignor Dennis she did not at first believe her prayer had gone out and returned already. She stared for a long time before finally deciding to go outside and confirm things for her own self. She walked stealthily, placing herself behind a tree near the gate, and as Pearline left Mother Lazarus took a closer look. The old woman knew it then; this was her prayer come back to her. *Yes indeedy*, she thought with relief, *this girl is the one.*

*

As if to make up for her lack of curiosity during those first six months, Pearline was now filled with a terrible impatience, and each time she repeated those three words that Mother Lazarus had said, that impatience grew. *It is time.* Pearline thought she knew time and its shapes: there were weekdays, and market day, and church day, and then weekdays again; and each day began with a rooster and ended with a chorus of frogs. The sun travelled across the sky, and men and women followed it on their own small journeys, leading cows to grass, hauling crocus bags of food from the ground, or just pressing on, pressing on like pilgrims. Most evenings found Pearline knitting, and so it seemed that night was a thing she made, with steady fingers.

But now time had unravelled and Pearline realised it was time that had been knitting her all along. She had no control over it – neither what it did nor what it would make of her. It could shift patterns just like that. She understood suddenly that, in the six months of her dull knitting, she had been heading towards something that would soon reveal itself, but she did not have a clue what this thing might be. And although half a year had passed quickly, the next Saturday could not come fast enough.

If she had suspected, however, that this particular Saturday, when it finally came, would be her last morning waking up in her rainbow room, her last morning spent in the village, and her last morning sitting at a table with her mother and father eating callaloo and yam farmed from their ground, she might not have been in such a hurry.

And if she had had any inkling that this new life would include, in quick succession, a child and the terrible thing that happened after ... well, she would definitely have slowed down. She would have savoured the yam, gloried in its smooth texture, its sweet taste. She would have gone over to the dutch pot for another portion. She would have sipped her tea instead of swallowing it so quickly it burnt her tongue. She would have hugged her mother goodbye. But she suspected no such thing, and when she finished her breakfast she gathered her knitting into a plastic bag and ran towards the leper colony.

✳

When she arrived, the morning mist had not yet risen from the valley and the three bungalows seemed to float as if in a dream. There was no Monsignor Dennis to greet Pearline. She walked round to the front of the bungalows and was surprised to see the gardens spread out like aprons before each one, full of aralia and bougainvillea.

She called out in a half-hearted way. She was enjoying this solitary moment on the grounds, observing the place for herself. The gardens were laid out in careful matrices; besides the aralia and the bougainvillea, there were also squares dedicated to tomatoes and ginger and onions. Near to the fence, there was a network of pumpkin vines.

'Hello ma'am?' she called out again, a little louder this time.

A broad patio extended from the middle bungalow, and on that deck was something that looked like a small city of rocking chairs. Rickety thrones. She began to feel comfortable.

'Hello!' she called a third time, and then there was a shout from inside.

'NO missis! Please, don't juuk me wid dat ting again, aaaaii-yeeeeee!!'

Pearline found herself on the ground, flat as a sheet. There was another scream. Something toppled over. Then there came the old woman's voice, firm.

'Hold steady Maas Johnny, you know we have to do this, hold steady!'

'Aaaaiyeeee!'

A silence stretched over the valley as if even the trees needed to take a breath after this assault. Seconds passed, and then, in the distance, a chicken squawked. It seemed a crude, indecorous sound, but it seemed to give permission to the landscape to carry on. The wind began to blow again and the valley regained its composure. Mother Lazarus stepped out from the middle bungalow, a long injection needle in her hand. She nodded to Pearline as if it were quite a natural thing to find her out there, her body still pressed to the earth.

'You come at a good time. I can show you around. But first follow me and let us get the porridge for them.'

Pearline's eyes were fixated on the needle, a bead of white liquid perched at its head.

Mother Lazarus looked on it and answered Pearline's unasked question.

'Chaulmoogra oil. They don't like it one bit, but is the ongly thing that help. Now come.'

Pearline stood up, slowly. She brushed the specks of dirt from her dress and followed the old woman into the farthest bungalow. She had expected the inside to be dark and musty but instead it was full of light. On the far wall where one might have expected windows or doors, there were big open slats. You could jump out straight into the garden. Two doors to the right seemed to lead to other rooms – bedrooms, she guessed – but the rest of the space was open. It seemed to be used as a kitchen and pantry of sorts. There were no shelves or cupboards, but everything was quite obviously in its place. Big sacks of cornmeal, rice and flour were in one corner; there was a sandalwood box for cured meat; small baskets of onions and garlic and scotch bonnet peppers were laid out carefully and unobtrusively on the floor, and there were also larger hampers for potatoes and yams; in another corner there were crocus bags of oranges and grapefruit, and towers of plates and pots rose from the mats of newspaper they were set upon. The only appliance was an enormous wood stove that seemed to sit in judgement over the whole kitchen. On top of the stove a black cauldron was already bubbling. Mother Lazarus went over and stirred, and then she began to speak.

'I feel as if I know you. But maybe this is not true at all. But see, I watch you come here every Saturday and I stand by the gate and I watch you leave. And I like what I been seeing.'

'Thank you, ma'am.'

'Yes indeedy, you have a sweetness to your spirit, child. I think you will like it here. Mmhm. I think you will.'

'Ma'am, I don't even know what this place is.'

'Mother Lazarus. You can call me Mother Lazarus. Yes. I taking too long to tell you the things you want to know. Forgive me.'

And, as if to take even longer, Mother Lazarus left the pot and ambled over to the tower of dishes. Her stumpy hands dislodged a stack of four bowls.

'Pearline,' she resumed, 'in a minute you will help me take this porridge over. You will meet them, but listen, you must understand that these people you is about to meet is just like anybody you have ever known. Yes indeedy. They probably won't look like anybody you have ever seen, but that is how it always is in this life, yes?'

'Yes, ma'am.'

'It is a horrible disease they have to bear. Sometimes it happen that their hands get so large it swallow up their fingers, one by one. The same thing happen with their toes – they just get loss inside their foot. You will see that their skin is very dry, like it bake in Gobi Desert, and no mount of coconut oil you rub them down with will change a thing. Mind you, you must rub them down all the same. And you must touch them, even though sometimes they

30

can't feel it. That is how it is with this disease, they get so they have no feeling.'

Pearline understood sickness as having bad feelings. She couldn't quite wrap her mind around having no feelings whatsoever.

'Excuse me please, ma'am, but what kind of sickness make you don't feel at all?'

The old woman shivered involuntarily, but did not answer Pearline directly.

'When you earn his confidence, which I guarantee you won't be long, you will draw long bench with Maas Paul and with his own mouth he will tell you all bout the woman, his own auntie, who grow him up. That woman would sometimes make him reach into a pot of boiling water or even hot oil to take out the food she was cooking for him. Think bout that for a little. If you see his hands now, they burn up bad bad. Black as tar. He never know what he was doing to himself, cause he never did feel it. It is a terrible, terrible disease.'

Pearline was now decidedly afraid.

'Ma'am, please, am I going to fall sick here?'

'And when it get bad bad,' Mother Lazarus continued, 'is when all the family decide they don't want to take care of them no more. That is when they have to come here. Their family might just throw them into the gully like they was a dead dog, or they might leave them at some church or take them to the doctor office and then run gone. Move house to make sure they don't ever see them again. That is how they end up here. You have some like Miss Lily who don't even have the use of her legs, but she come here on her own backside. It take her one week. She drag herself up the mountain and then drag herself down the valley. When she reach here, her batty tear up like backra done whip her. And she do all that so she could end up at a place where people don't look on her with scorn. I hope you hearing what I is saying. When you help me take this porridge over, don't open up your two eyes at them like you shock.'

31

'Yes, ma'am, but ...'

'But you must not look away neither. That is worse.'

'Yes, ma'am, I won't look away. But beg you please to tell me ...'

'Mother Lazarus, you are to call me Mother Lazarus. People don't like to call me Agatha cause I so old they think to call me Agatha would be too familiar. But I don't mind it. Just don't call me ma'am cause that make me sound like I is a schoolteacher or something, and I is not that.'

'Yes, Mother Lazarus.'

The old woman finished ladling out the bowls of porridge. She walked over to Pearline and took her soft young hands in her old wrinkly ones. 'You must not worry your head one little bit, my child. You is in no danger of catching it. The people who live here is lepers.'

Mother Lazarus looked on the young woman for a moment, and then nodded as if she had made some decision.

Pearline swallowed.

'I already set up one of those rooms in the back for you, so I hope you will want to stay. You see, Pearline, I know they is going to like you, and I sure you is going to like them, and that is all that is important. Now come, take two of those bowls and let us go over. Remember now, my child, don't stare.'

So Pearline followed Mother Lazarus back across the garden, up the steps of the middle bungalow and then inside. And poor thing, she could not help it. She stared.

※

She had been prepared for the deformities. These did not surprise her. In fact, she thought they might have been worse. It was true, she saw hands without fingers, and coarsened skin that reminded her of alligators, and she saw a crevice in the middle of a face

32

where there should have been a nose, and she saw stumps, and she saw charred limbs. But none of this – the scars, the missing digits, the hardened skin, affected Pearline seriously. It was not the bodies themselves that she was staring at, how they each had, in some way, failed the persons they belonged to. Instead she stared at what was on those bodies, wrapped around their feet and their hands. It was the 'ongly-thats' she had knitted.

For the first time Pearline realised she had been making bandages. And the display struck her, all at once, as more beautiful than her rainbow room. How strange, she thought; she had made the bandages in a kind of stupor, but now she was impressed by the nobility of the undertaking. She, a bandage maker. She placed the two porridge bowls on the floor and walked over to a bald-headed man she would later know as Maas Paul. She ran a finger along the length of the bandage around his foot. Her index finger trailed the circle until it could twist no farther.

'How it feel, sir?'

In truth, Maas Paul could hardly feel a thing. Feelings were especially dead in his feet. But he liked how the bandages covered them up, those two things that had embarrassed him for so many years. And he even thought, if only they could cover more, cover up his whole self, wrap him like an Egyptian mummy, then he would be ecstatic. So he knew how the bandages made him feel – less embarrassed about his body, and proud that a young woman whom he had never met before could have been drawn to his feet, and without the shadow of pity crossing her features, had looked at them as if they were beautiful.

'The bandages, miss? Oh, they feel very lovely. Very lovely indeed.'

'Young miss,' said another man sitting across from him. 'Come feel my own. I bet you find them even lovelier.'

'You all acting like a bunch of schoolboys already.' Mother Lazarus reprimanded them, but she was smiling.

'Stay out of this, old woman, and make the young miss come over and feel my bandages.'

It was then that a woman whose head had been diligently buried in a book looked up and spoke.

'So is it you who has made these bandages for us?'

Pearline understood instinctively that this was a woman who did not speak often, and she guessed correctly that this was the Miss Lily who had dragged her arse up and then down the mountain. She was the only female in the group of four. It was she who had the crevice in the middle of her face where there once had been a nose.

'Y-yes ma'am,' Pearline stammered. 'Is me that make them.'

'Well, my dear, they are lovely. No, more than lovely. They are beautiful.'

The residents of the leper colony did not know about Pearline's disastrous day at the market six months earlier; they did not know about the shoe vendor, Maizy, who had accused Pearline of making a doily that had hog-killing properties; they did not know about the doubts of Pearline's mother; they did not know about everyone else in the world who had called everything she had ever knitted ugly. So they did not know what it meant to her when they said they thought her bandages were beautiful. They simply watched as tear after tear welled up and then rolled down her cheeks.

Pearline stood there, in this great tide of sentiment, and made another decision then and there. She had already taken the trail down to the leper colony. Now she decided she would stay. And what was more, she was going to turn it into a beautiful place. She was going to make a colony of many colours.

an instalment of a testimony spoken to the wind

Shhhhhhhhh

WHAT THIS MAN taking his own sweet time to tell you is that Pearline Portious is dead. She is dead and buried as many years and as many days as I have had breath. I never know her and never before I read so much bout her as I is reading now. They say she died quiet, but she must have been in plenty pain. Bless her. When I was a little girl I used to sit on the veranda at number 35, when the sun was low and the sky was like a blood-red scarf wrap round the mountains, and I try to learn myself to knit. They tell me this was the gift my mama had. They tell me she could turn string into sweaters and blankets and doilies and bandages. I wanted this gift to pass on to me, so I asked her spirit, if it was out there, to guide my fingers. But the two needles did always slip from my hands, or the string would slip off the needles, or I would never make the knots right. I was no good at it. And sometimes I wonder if that did break her heart, that I couldn't be her daughter in such a way as that.

Shhhhhhhhh

Let me tell you all I really know of Miss Pearline. She was a woman like the wind, for just as no one knoweth where the wind come from so too I cannot tell you who was Pearline's people, or in which part she did grow, or anything of that sort. She find her way to Queen Margaret Drive on an ordinary morning asking for work. People would do that in those days – walk on street, a small stone in their hands, and knock on gates. When the boss

36

lady or the boss man come out to answer the *ping ping ping*, the person at the gate would have to talk out their résumé right then and there. *Ma'am, sir, I is fit and able to do any kind of work you may have — washing, cleaning, cooking, whatever it is.* So it happen that when Pearline came knocking on Queen Margaret Drive she got lucky. Mother Lazarus really did need help for true. So Pearline move in and she work at that house for little over a year. Maybe she would have continued but as I tell you, on the day that I made my way into this world, birth pain hit Pearline hard, and she made her own way out. No newspaper did carry that story. It was not written down in any book. Not a thing has been written bout Pearline Portious. She never important to the world, and so the world ongly write down her name three times: the first, on her birth paper; the second, on mine; and the third, on her death paper.

Shhhhhhhhh

I was never short of mothers though. First, there was Mother Lazarus and I probably did look more like she than I could ever look like Pearline. You see, they tell me that this Pearline Portious used to be a pretty young woman, but I have never been what anyone could call pretty. And they tell me her skin was the colour of nutmeg and that her fingers was long and slender, and it was her fingers that you would always notice, because they was always busy doing this or that. My fingers is short and stumpy, like Mother Lazarus's; and me and Mother Lazarus have skin like the deepest part of night. Schoolboys used to say you can't see Adamine until she smile. But this Mr Writer Man who is writing my story, I must give him his due, for what he say bout Mother Lazarus is correct. She

37

was a short old woman with big hair, and always wearing two shirts. It is only one place where his description fall short, for I forget to tell him bout the freckles on her face. It was like God did sprinkle black pepper over it. And also, it is true, she did smell of oranges and lemongrass and powder, but that is the only way to describe the perfume she did always make for herself. Old as she was, Mother Lazarus had her vanities.

Shhhhhhhhh

The one lesson that woman tried hard to learn me was this – to believe in miracles. And in angels. And in demons. And in the devil. And I still believe in all of those things. But she said I shouldn't bother believing in no God. She said it made not a lick of sense to believe in someone who did not believe in you. She said his eye was ongly on the sparrow, it was not turned towards poor people. Mother Lazarus said there was evil and good and all kinds of magic in the world, but is best we learn how to use those things for our own selves than wait around on any God to do things for we. I did wonder why her heart was so hard against God, and then one night she tell me. It was a night when the room was so hot that I couldn't fall asleep. Her voice reach me from the darkness. *Ada, you sleeping?* I tell her I was awake, and just so she start to tell me the story. I had not too long turned twelve and maybe in her own way Mother Lazarus decide it was time to give me a warning:

Ada, when I was just a girl, bout the time when I had achieved the

38

same age you have just achieved yourself, I went to the river to catch janga-shrimp. When I catch enough janga to fill my skirt, I begin to walk back home. I had to make my way through the cane, and the sun was like a fire above me. Nowhere on earth does the sun shine hotter or more evilous than it does when it shine over cane. Yes indeedy. Well, I was walking through that sunhot when I hear like clipclopclipclop behind me and I feel the dust rising up everywhere like when a flour bag drop and bust open. I never have to look behind me to know it was the devil. I don't mean to say this man who was riding up behind me had horns or that him did have a tail or goat feet, but there was just something evil in this man. I should tell you now, it was my own brother. Yes child. He did born from the same woman as me, but this boy was also a creole, for his papa was a white man. So he did live in the big house with his big important family. But is like him never satisfy with that. Is like him did want to be full white, and he think that to be white mean you have to step on black people. Whenever he ride out on his horse, he would call out to them that was his own cousins and brothers and sisters. Even his mother. My mother. Him would say, look on all you, you ugly set o nayga! It come a time when he even start riding with a whip. The time of cane and whip was done. Massa Day did done, but is like this man wish in his heart that such things did not done. And it was this man who did ride up behind me with his whip. He jump down from his horse and I start to bawl right then and there, Jesus save me! Jesus save me! because I was a fool. Neither Jesus nor nobody else did save me, and right there under the hot sun, mongst the hard cane and the stinking dead janga, that man make a woman out of me long long before I was ready to be a woman. And after he done that thing that man will do unto a woman, and him ride off with him whip, I know that he had put a baby inside me. I feel it. So I stay right where I was. I never stir a muscle. I never call unto Jesus neither, cause I learn that lesson fast. But I speak unto my own belly with my own girl voice — I say I not having no pickney! I not having no pickney! And I keep on keep on keep on saying it until

39

it become true, until I feel my insides get hard, and I start to bleed. I almost pass out right there and it was the next morning before anybody find me. I never been able to have a pickney since that time, even when I was a young woman and was ready for a child. And I tell you what, my dear Ada — I used to be vex with God for not answering me that day. Yes indeedy. But I was even more vex with myself for speaking unto my belly like that, blocking it up so strong that even me could not unblock it later.

That is another way in which I have become like Mother Lazarus, for I don't have no children of my own and it is too late now. My womb been closed a long long time, like a shop that never had enough custom. But I learn something about Mother Lazarus that night. Her words did really have all the power of Creation in them; for I tell you something else: when I was born and my mother did lay dead on that bed, it was Mother Lazarus who spake unto herself saying, this child need me. I cannot die for fifteen more years. And so said, so done. She lived fifteen years to the day, till she was 105. On my very birthday she decide at last it was time to dead. It was the 18th of March.

Shhhhhhhhh

Everything that is important to me happen on that day. On the 18th of March I was born. On the 18th of March my mother dead. On the 18th of March, Mother Lazarus lie down on her cot, pleased as Miss Thomas puss, and dead. On the 18th of March I get the calling. I did run from the calling at first. I know it was God, and I did

40

scared. I did want to hide in cave like Elijah, or inside a fishbelly like Jonah. Deep down I always believe in the Saviour – no matter what Mother Lazarus did try to learn me – but I did believe her when she say he was not interested in people such as we. So I never know what business God, all on a sudden, want to have with me. I put my fingers in my ears, but this calling was like an earthquake inside my head that no bush tea could cure. I finally pick myself up one night and run straight to the Revival Church. I step into the room and the Captain spin down from his pulpit and ask me 'what is thy name young lady?' I tell him, and is like the sound of my name was an alabaster jar broken. The whole room gasp, and the place was full of a sweet and holy fragrance. The women start to dance wild and they sing and cry and spin and dip, and they shout Glory Glory Glory. Poor me don't understand none of this commotion. The Captain man pull me aside and he give me directions to the Bishopess's yard. He say go quick, girl child, for she has been calling unto you for days and nights.

Shhhhhhhhh

Listen: it was Bishopess Herbert who did plant herself under a guava tree. It was Bishopess Herbert who said she wasn't leaving that spot come hell or high water. And she bear the scorn of her neighbours the way Jesus bear the cross. She was calling out this name that was put onto her spirit: Adamine. She never meet me in her whole life, but in her spirit she know I was out there, and she wait for me with love the size of a lion. She stand up in that yard for days, in front of the shanty house. And people laugh at her. They say she lose her mind. One man even

41

try to chase her out of the yard, saying she was nothing but an obeah woman. But she stay there calling out Adamine, Adamine. And finally, O lamb of God, I did come, I come. When she see me, the Bishopess embrace me like the hundredth lamb that did loss and finally reach back to the flock. So after Agatha Lazarus, she was now my second mother. Is she who learn me how to listen; learn me how to make God's voice my own; learn me how to be full up of the '61 spirit and give warning. Is she who make me to know that my calling was to be a Warner Woman. And maybe when I come to England and they lock me up for madness, maybe I get other mothers then – for the matron and all the nurses treat me like I was a little pickney, but I not studying that right now.

Shhhhhhhhh

As for fathers, I have none but the Lord. I never find out who my earthly father was. I more sure of who it was not. 1) It was not Monsignor Dennis. I get his story piece piece from Mother Lazarus and Miss Lily and Maas Paul. It is true that you would always find him in the garden, but you would never catch him doing work himself. According to them he was not the type to stoop over no bush and put eggshells in the dirt. Instead he was always standing up over the yardboy. The yardboy change like how some people change underwear. It was always these tall, mawga boys and Monsignor Dennis would stand up over them and instruct them to sweep here, or to plant this or plant that. Mother Lazarus say the Monsignor did hate her because she always come to him when he was out there giving his instructions and labrishing, talking away like his tongue did catch fire. Mother Lazarus put the question to me, *what else I could do, child? I couldn't go up to him at no other time because that was all him do the livelong day.* Mother Lazarus tell me when him see her coming he would say, *Miss Lazarus, don't you see I'm out here talking to so-and-so.* Sometimes she hold her tongue but other times she answer him brave and say, *yes, I can see. And I can hear too. Even cin the wee hours of the morning, I hear things you think I can't hear.* Mother Lazarus tell me that whenever she say something like that the yardboy would start doing pure stupidness, like he was nervous, and Monsignor Dennis would turn twenty shades of red that not even the sun could turn him. 2) My father was not the Jamaican hero, Alexander Bustamante. Everybody did wish they was the child of that tall brown man, especially after he march with the workers downtown, and when the police come to shoot black people it was Bustamante who climb up on the statue of Queen Victoria and tear off his shirt and show them his chest, and say you will have to shoot me first. After he say that, everybody wish their chest was as big and as broad as his, and so they call him Father Busta. They said he was father of the nation. And maybe that's why I get his name, because I never have a real father, so they just name me after the man who was father to everybody. 3) My father was not Mr Mac, the driver who come on Saturday evenings with supplies, and leave with my mother. Mother Lazarus tell me Mr Mac was a good-looking fellow in those days, before he drink a river's worth of beer and rum and put on plenty weight. Mr Mac tell me himself that all my mother wanted from him was a drive into town and so he would drop her there on Saturday nights, but all the try that he did try to take it farther, the most he ever get from her was a kiss on the cheek. 4) My father was not a leper, not Maas Paul, 5) nor Maas Johnson, 6) nor Maas Johnny. When she was pregnant these three men was suddenly cool towards my mother, like they never business bout her again. Her belly was a reproof unto them, for all of them was a little bit in love with my mother, but her belly make them know they wasn't quite man enough for she.

Shhhhhhhhh

More than likely my father was a simple, forgettable man. I imagine my mother did meet him on a Saturday night when she had gone into town. I try to imagine her in that big city, Pearline Portious, as beautiful as the Rose of Sharon, mesmerised by all them lights. I see her walking into a dance and every man's eye is suddenly set upon her, watching with man-hunger while she dance up a storm and sweat trickle down into her bosom. She would always find her own way home, but it happen that one night she must have taken a long way, cause she come back pregnant. No shame in that. She was her own big woman after all. But who it was that did the breeding I cannot tell you, because I did not ever ask it of Pearline Portious, because she was not around to tell me.

A Night So Long in Coming

If you had been around back then in 1941, you would not have spotted in Mother Lazarus the usual signs of fatigue. There were no droopy eyes, no sluggish movements, no yawns the size and decibel of a roar. She displayed no symptoms, and yet more than anything else Mother Lazarus wanted to sleep. She had not slept for eighty years.

Her insomnia started at the age of ten when a traumatic event — to put it plainly, a rape — kept her wide awake for seven days straight. When Agatha did not return home one evening, her mother began to wail and wail, and the sound was like a siren over the cane. Every woman responded by pushing her man out of bed, if he hadn't already risen by himself, and sent him towards the wailing to see what had happened. The men formed themselves into a search party and told Agatha's mother to stay put, understanding even then that it would not be good for her to find her own child, see the possibly mangled and lifeless body and receive a shock great enough to send her to the grave as well.

It was dawn before the men found Agatha. One man immediately vomited up the tea and bread he had eaten before setting out, for Agatha was lying in a pool of congealed blood and mud. Two men picked her up as gently as their calloused hands could manage. She didn't make a sound, didn't resist, and if it were not for her eyes that even then were wide open, and her chest, which continued to rise and fall, they would have believed her dead.

They marched back to the wattle-and-daub house in which her mother waited. She saw the search party coming from afar and could make out the body of her daughter dangling from their arms. At first she pressed herself as deep into the house as she could, trying to slip into its shadows. 'Lord Jesus!' she shouted. 'Not mi daughter. Lord Jesus, take the case!'

'Take heart, Mumma,' the men called back, 'take heart. She is alive.'

They had to say it a few more times before the words finally made sense. At last the mother lifted herself from the wall and ran towards the group. One man stepped out to block her. He held her in his arms.

'Let me go. I need to see her. I need to know that she alive for true.'

'Take heart, Mumma. We tell you that she is alive. But we find her in a bad bad way.'

'Let me see her,' the mother cried, but she was shaking, her strength leaving her.

'We find her in a bad way, Mumma. Her panty did tear off and fling to one side, and ...'

'Don't tell me. Don't tell me.'

'Mumma, we have to tell you before you see her ... I sorry. The whole of her pum-pum was out-a-door. We never did want to see the young girl like that at all, but that is how we find her. Mumma, don't faint on we now. Keep strength and take heart. I tell you she is alive. But she in a bad way for true.'

So it was, the little girl was delivered into her mother's arms and for one whole week she did not blink. Her unfocused eyes made people think she was staring into another world; they worried that the child was looking at her own death and walking towards it. They tried to tempt her back to the land of the living through a number of ways: by the strategic placement of small mirrors all around her (what the obeah man had told them to do, advising them that the child needed to be surprised by her own reflection); by throwing red string in front of her, then drawing it away slowly (what the myal woman had told them to do, advising them that an evil spirit in the form of a cat had possessed the girl and needed to be lured out); by walking round the house seven times and banging a pot with a wooden spoon (what the old brother-man who lived in the cave by the river had told them to do, advising them that this was the sure way of frightening bad spirits).

But none of it worked. She had become a zombie – the living dead. Agatha's mother was inconsolable.

'When I find that dutty bwoy who do this evil unto my daughter, him owna sister, I going to kill him! With my own two hands I going to kill him.'

Her mother took time off from the sugar factory where she worked. She stayed at home and held Agatha in her big hands and sang to her: 'Come back, Gatha. Come back yah. Water come a mi eye. Come back, Gatha. Come back yah. Water come a mi eye.'

And maybe what the obeah man, and the myal woman, and the brother-man who lived in the cave by the river had not bothered to say, but which everyone knew, was true – that there were some things, some evils, some curses in this world, that will take either three, or seven, or nine days to cure. For it was on the seventh day of her mother's song that Agatha finally relaxed in her embrace and the fear that had prevented her eyelids from descending finally lifted.

Some of the damage, however, was deeper and could not be cured. Agatha was now able to blink; she could close her eyes whenever she wanted, but the ability to fall asleep had been lost. Agatha would lie on her cot each night only to please her mother. She would close her eyes and breathe deeply. But she never truly drifted into sleep. She was acutely conscious of every passing minute, every second that ticked away, and in this way she began to learn the exact sounds of darkness, the precise measure of night.

47

She knew what belonged where and when. So if she heard, for instance, a particular flutter of wings in the daytime, she would look up startled and ask of the creature, Mr Rat-bat, what are you doing up at this time? This is not your hour.

For eighty years Agatha Lazarus had lived in this somniphobic state. Life had been one everlasting day. And then there came a strange moment in 1941.

She had been in the middle of complaining to Monsignor Dennis, explaining to him that they were out of sugar, out of rice, out of antiseptic, but most humiliatingly, out of tissue. She said that she didn't understand why they had to be completely out of things before they could be replaced, and that furthermore ... And then she stopped, in mid-flow. She had suddenly become aware of a new sensation in her body. A deep scowl clouded her face and even Monsignor Dennis asked whether she was all right. She nodded her head and said yes, yes, she was fine and continued with her protests. But it was from that moment on that she became slightly distracted. This new sensation was curious. What she felt was a slight tingling in one of her little fingers. It lasted for two days and then, instead of disappearing, it jumped straight across her body to the other little finger. It was as if a swarm of tiny insects were buzzing inside those two digits. The insects began to grow in number and to move out. Some migrated to the other fingers, her thumbs, and soon her entire hand was tingling. Eventually they travelled farther, across her shoulders, up to her neck, then to her face, where they seemed to be most particularly drawn to her eyelids. They stayed there for so long that she thought they had settled permanently, but then one morning a whole battalion plunged deep into her stomach, then to her hips, and then, at last, to her feet and her toes.

Not having felt this sensation for eighty years, she did not recognise it as acute fatigue. But soon her thoughts began to lose their solidity, changing form as quickly as ghosts. She would look at a tree, for instance, consider its bark, and this would make her think of the colour brown and people who were the colour of trees, which in turn made her think of people as mahogany or cedar or pine or blue mahoe or even the poisonous manchineel. Then all at once she would become worried about what kind of tree she was and where she should be planted. She would touch her hair and think *my leaves have turned grey! Who ever heard of grey leaves!* And finally she knew that this was the beginning of what people called a dream. After eighty years, she had regained the ability to fall asleep. So she smiled. She was going to do it after all. One night when she really wanted to, she would do it. But she understood, just as her waking hours had felt like an eternity, so too would her sleep be eternal. She would never wake up from it, and this made her smile all the more. Mother Lazarus had begun to fear that she might never die, and so the fact of an irreversible state of sleep into which she could descend whenever she wanted came as something of a relief.

Still, things had to be done correctly. Arrangements had to be made. Someone had to be hired. So this is what Pearline Portious was for Mother Lazarus – a part of her big plan. She knew that a night would come soon when, after everyone had fallen asleep, she would step outside into the night breeze and slowly walk the mile-long perimeter of the colony. She would nod goodbye instead of hello to the bats and the peeniwallies and the patoos and the moths with their enormous faith, always fluttering around excitedly as if tonight was the night when they would finally reach the moon. After she had checked that everything and everyone was in their rightful place, she would go back inside, into her room, and she would put on a fresh nightgown. It would be a nightgown she had never worn before. She would blow out the candle, climb into her bed and pull the sheet up over her. She would rest her head on the pillow and look one last time into the comforting darkness, and then she would surrender herself to it. She would close her eyes, knowing that she would never open them again.

✳

Here is a theory you may have begun to turn around in your head: could it be that the sudden whisking off of Monsignor Dennis to Kingston was also part of Agatha Lazarus's elaborate plan to fall asleep? Could it be that the old woman had spoken indiscreetly and caused a rumour to travel all the way to Kingston, which in turn caused Monsignor Dennis to have to leave the colony, following that rumour to where it had landed in the ears of his superiors? Could it be that when he left the colony before Pearline came, he was not simply taking his yearly vacation; it was not that he went back to England to visit friends and family? Could it really be that it was the old woman's meddling that had caused his departure, as if she was trying to get him out of the way to make sure that Pearline's arrival was unobstructed? You may wonder these things because of how easily Pearline slipped into life at the colony, and how broken a man Albert Dennis was when he returned.

Well, supposing you had the time and the money and the inclination, you could actually follow this story right back to its beginning. You could book yourself a ticket and go to Jamaica. Although, where does a story really begin? And what would you do on the island?

Perhaps you could start by going to the Registrar's Office in Spanish Town. You might want to look for birth and death certificates. This would be a mistake. You would quickly realise that you just don't have that kind of time. The queue at the Registrar's Office stretches on for what looks like days. And even if you were lucky enough to reach the counter you would then find three women with tight perms and tighter lips, who would speak animatedly and at length to each other about a show called Royal Palm Estate (you have never heard of it), but would look at you contemptuously above the rim of their glasses if you dared to say, Excuse me, excuse me please.

They would answer, One minute, sir. And then take fifteen.

And if you were so lucky as to be granted an audience, eventually, after your six hours of trying to get to the counter, and you were smart enough to measure your tone and still be polite, the nice women with the tight perms and tighter lips would ask you if you had brought a letter stamped by a justice of the peace, and your passport, and a proof of address, and a police record, and the required fee made out as a manager's cheque, and the fifteen other useless things you should have brought with you, and if you had forgotten any one of these things which you inevitably would have, they would lift their unimpressed brows and dismiss you.

'Sorry, sir, we can't help.'

And even if the next day you had everything, you would find out then that records are never located quickly in Jamaica. That files are unfiled. That some files do not exist. That to look for it yourself would mean being led to an enormous warehouse, to boxes and boxes exploding with records, piled to the ceiling and running on for miles. You would decide then, quite wisely, that maybe the story need not start here after all.

Next you could go the Office of the Archdiocese of Spanish Town. You would have to tell all manner of lies for half an hour straight, hoping the Lord would not strike you down for the brazenness of it all, before you finally gained access to the records detailing the activities of the diocese between 1940 and 1960. You would sit alone in a dusty room, taking down ledger after ledger, leafing through their pages hoping to find something, anything, relating to the leper colony that the church once ran.

You would maybe find a little piece of information here, and another little piece there, but nothing that brought the people back to life. And mostly you would squint, and then squint some more over the records because everything had been written down in pencil, much of it was now faded, or smudged into illegibility, or occasionally erased. You would realise then that this is what history is – a series of smudges, a ream of blank paper, a catalogue of events lost to the moments in which they happened.

But now your time in Jamaica is running short so you decide to follow a hunch and search for a man by the name of Ernie McIntyre. When you find this Mr McIntyre he will insist that you simply call him Mr Mac.

'Even my mother did call me Mr Mac,' he tells you.

He will be an old man of an incredible size – a belly so big that his shirt cannot be buttoned; he'll also have a great big head, and a sprawling set of buttocks, all of which will make you wonder if he can squeeze it all into the front seat of the Lada taxi he still drives for a living.

You have found him in a shopping plaza where he waits for passengers during the day, and as you walk towards him he will shuffle around to open the front passenger door. *'Where to, young man?'*

You wave your hands. *'Cheers, sir, but no thank you,'* and he will look at you with annoyance.

You explain then that you don't need a taxi, but you have in fact been looking for him, and you are willing to pay him for his time. And if you tell him then that what you really want is to know about the leper colony that was once in Stone Hill, St Catherine, Mr Mac will look up with a start.

'The leper colony? But how you even know bout that, massa? That is long time history. Long long time, when I was a young strapping man like yuself. Once upon a time I used to drive people up there to see the ruins, and I hope you doesn't take no offence when I say this, but it was always white people who was interested in going up there.'

You are so excited to have found a witness, but you try not to ask him everything at once. You start, of course, with the Original Pearline Portious.

He squints his eyes and shakes his head a little as if to loosen a memory. 'Yes, I remember she. Pretty young thing. She was one of those that dead too young. Long, long before her time.' He will proceed to tell you everything that he remembers about her, but in all honesty it is less than you had hoped for.

'Mother Lazarus?' you ask hopefully.

'Yes, of course. She I remember plain plain. She was old as Methuselah as they say. Is she who did keep things going. And when she dead, everything just fall to pieces. The poor people them just dead straight off, and the place go right back to forest.'

'Monsignor Dennis?'

'That white man wasn't a nice fellow at all, at all. Oh sorry, sorry sir, don't get me wrong now. I got nothing gainst white people, but the man you ask me bout just now, Missa Dennis, yes? Him was a crabbit kind of fellow. And then, poor thing, his age did come upon him sudden and him wasn't no use to nobody no more.'

'And the Warner Woman?'

'Well I never know her as no Warner Woman. She did become that later on. A very powerful Warner Woman. But when I know her she was just a little girl who did live mongst the lepers. She never pretty neither. Sorry to say, but is true. Ada she did name. Just a regular little pickney. I never pay her much mind then. But is she who did leave them to dead. I blame it all on her. She leave them to die there on their lonesome, and then she become big Warner Woman, and her name did get large in this country, and then just like so, she drop off the face of the earth.'

You want to explain that Adamine only dropped off the face of Jamaica; that she reappeared in England where, as she put it, she was made to till a hard ground. But you do not say this, and almost an hour later you are still trying to pry yet more information from Mr Mac, to get him out of the reverie into which he so easily slips and is then lost to you. You remind him again that you are in Jamaica to do research. Yes, you tell him, a story you are writing, and that your publishers have paid for you to come here. You tell him again that you have travelled a long way. So please, what else might he be able to tell you? He will then sigh.

'Lawd, poor old man like me, I don't have no big knowledge to tell you. I never know them people all that well. But once upon a time I used to drive people up there to Stone Hill. I can take you if you wants. And you know it was always white people was interested in going up there? I show them where I did find the last body – the woman who just dead in her wheelchair. Before my very eyes she did dead. No way I can ever forget that. And always is white people who want to know these things.'

But you have heard this already. Several times in fact. 'Actually, I'm not white,' you might begin to explain resentfully, but you know Mr Mac would simply continue as if you had said nothing.

'Don't get me wrong sir, I not prejudiced against your kind, but a black man never ask me about those lepers.' And he would start his story all over again.

So this is what you would have left Jamaica with: not a single record from the Registrar's Office; nothing substantial from the church's archives; and a taped conversation with an old man, partially senile, whose story keeps looping on itself and never really goes anywhere. But perhaps in all of this you would take away the most valuable lesson: that to write down a story from the past, you must be loose with the facts; you must only be true to the truth.

✳

Perhaps no one will ever know the extent of Mother Lazarus's plans to fall asleep – how much plotting was involved, if rumours had been maliciously sown and people sent away. The point is this – Pearline Portious arrived at the leper colony. And her arrival was like sunshine after too many years of darkness. The place changed. And when Monsignor Dennis returned, it was as if he had not come back with all of himself. That

54

afternoon he grunted something which may have been *hello*, or *piss off*, and then he turned around and went straight back to his gardening. Mother Lazarus shook her head sadly and said, 'Is age. It has suddenly come upon him.' Of the tall, intimidating gentleman Pearline had met on the first day, she would see only brief glimpses, a faint resemblance.

Pearline spent each day on the patio with the four residents. There was Maas Paul, the oldest of the group, with his burnt limbs – a timid gentleman with a sweet spirit. Pearline knitted sky-blue bandages for him, and told him she thought he was the kind of man to whom birds would come willingly. There was Maas Johnson, the official joker of the group, a once-handsome man with skin the colour of Mandeville dirt, burnt red, who did nothing but flirt with Pearline Portious, assuring her that although he had lost six fingers, he hadn't lost the part of him that was most important; and there was Maas Johnny who was really Maas Johnson as well – he was Maas Johnson's little brother, so they called him Maas Johnny to distinguish the two. Pearline made orange and red bandages for the pair, because she felt their skin was already the colour of fire. And finally there was Miss Lily, the one woman, with no nose and no legs. She sat in her wheelchair each day, her head buried in the novel *Jane Eyre* which she kept reading from cover to cover. As soon as she finished the book, she would go right back to page one and start over. Pearline made deep purple bandages for Miss Lily, because she thought the woman sat there like a queen. Noble.

And so she fulfilled her promise. She transformed the place into a colony of colours. She made the lepers beautiful. And because of her presence, laughter would now occasionally rise up from the once quiet valley, and the people in the mountain wondered if the terrible sickness had finally left the place.

But it was Mother Lazarus especially who became a different person. She began to close her eyes and sing. Every day it was the same song.

> Soon and very soon
> I am going to see the King
> Soon and very soon
> I am going to see the King
> Soon and very soon
> I am going to see the King
> Hallelujah, Hallelujah
> I am going to see the King

It surprised everyone, this song of faith, so they asked her about it.

'You always say you don't believe in God, Mother Lazarus, but now you singing that sankey every day like you suddenly find Jesus.'

'I not singing to no God,' she answered honestly. 'I just singing to something I been waiting on for a long time. And it soon come. Soon and very soon.'

'Eh eh!' exclaimed Maas Johnson. 'Mother Lazarus look like she soon going to get man in her bed. You think that old woman easy?'

Everyone laughed, but Mother Lazarus continued singing, and every day it was like this. Laughing and songs; laughter and songs.

Then one day they noticed that Pearline's belly had started to grow.

Mother Lazarus paused in her song.

'Pearline child, is pregnant you really pregnant?'

Pearline smiled sheepishly. 'It look so, don't it?'

'Yes, it look so,' Mother Lazarus agreed.

Agatha Lazarus started her song again but there was a sadder note in it, if you listened very closely, as if she knew the 'soon' that she was singing would not be as soon as she had hoped. Indeed, she decided she would have to wait on this child to be born. She figured she had already been awake for eighty years and she could wait just a little while longer. Nine months is nothing at all. That

56

is what she said to herself. And true enough, the months passed quickly.

✳

On 18 March 1942, everyone was sitting in their chairs. Pearline had begun the new task of sewing clothes for the baby that was coming. Then, in the middle of a stitch, she winced and leaned forward. Miss Lily noticed.

'You OK there, Pearline?'

Pearline shook her head.

'Mercy me, what is the matter, child?'

'I think it is time,' Pearline said, her voice little more than a whisper. She gritted her teeth and let her needles fall from her hands. She was now gripping the sides of the chair tightly and rocking in a pool of pre-birth water. A contraction raced through her body, an earthquake ripping her in two. She shouted now for the whole valley to hear. 'It is time! It is time! Lord have mercy on a sinner like me, it is time!'

Here are some other theories you may have begun to toss around:

- that maybe Pearline Portious finally understood these three words. It is time. Maybe she understood that time was always changing its shape and that one day it would assume a shape that would no longer include her. To say, 'it is time' was therefore a kind of prayer, a shorthand way of saying something much larger, like – it is time that occasionally smiles on us, it is time that eventually frowns on us, it is time that we are always bowed before and asking for more of, it is time that will one day leave us.

- that maybe in the excitement of all the screaming and the water-breaking, Mother Lazarus had kept a steady head. She had not been distracted. And so she, who was supposed to understand the importance of cleanliness, really did wash her hands, really

did put the water on to boil, really did lay fresh sheets on the
bed, all the things a midwife would have known to do.

- that maybe if Mother Lazarus had indeed done these things
  (which, let us be honest, is unlikely), the Original Pearline
  Portious would have lived, would have been around to raise her
  daughter.
- that maybe this could have been a very different story.

But tell me, what is the use of all these maybes when Pearline
Portious did, in fact, die?

In the room where they finally took her, Mother Lazarus was
shouting like a cheerleader.

'Push, girl! Push!'

So Pearline pushed.

'Yes, I see it coming, girl. Push. Come on, just a little more.'

So Pearline pushed a little more.

'The head, I holding the head! You doing good, girl. Push now!
Push!'

And Pearline's eyes began to flutter.

'Come Pearline, come!'

Pearline gasped.

'A little more!'

Pearline's eyes were suddenly flung open, as if she had seen
something spectacular. And they stayed like that. Open. Lifeless.

But Mother Lazarus continued 'Push, Pearline, push!'

And now Mother Lazarus was pulling. She reached inside the girl
and started to pry the baby out with her own hands.

'Good job, Pearline mi girl! One last push!'

And Mother Lazarus herself pulled the baby right out. The infant
and the old woman hollered together; the first protesting at the
indignity of being thrust into the light, the other with exhaustion
and joy. Pearline's hand dangled off the bed, and it was this, more
than her absent heartbeat, more than her discontinued breath, that
became the irrefutable evidence that Pearline was no more, that she

had fallen outside of time and departed from her own body.

From the doorway Maas Paul and Maas Johnson saw the hand and they started weeping over it, as if no other part of Pearline had died. As if they knew it would take time and strength to grieve over her face, and then her legs, and then her knees, because sometimes grief is so great it must be divided.

Mother Lazarus remained oblivious.

'Pearline, you have a little girl. Look on this little girl you have.'

Only then did she look around. She saw now the glazed eyes; she noticed the hand.

'Pearline?'

She recognised on Pearline's face the kind of sleep she herself had been longing for, a sleep that had been so long in coming.

'Pearline! Don't you do this to me, young lady. It is not your turn. Is not your turn!'

Agatha Lazarus found out then that there is a moment when a dream is so utterly crushed, that instead of withering the dreamer will explode. Such is the ache and violence of disappointment. She began punching the dead body of Pearline Portious. Mother Lazarus opened the palms of her hands and slapped Pearline's lifeless face.

'Wake up. Wake up now. This not fair, Pearline. Wake up or else I kill you.'

But soon Mother Lazarus was sobbing. For no matter how many times she punched the body, or how many times she slapped the face, or how loudly she shouted, or how seriously she threatened, or how much water dripped from her eyes, Pearline Portious would not wake up. And this time it did not matter how desperate her prayer was; her desperation was not powerful enough to bring back the dead.

So there it was, this room, and inside it was a dead body and all the stinking mess of birth: blood and shit and mucus. And a baby was wailing. And an old woman was beating her chest. No one dared step into this strange vortex, this room like an obeah curse.

They left it to Mother Lazarus to bring her own self back.

She had to say to herself, 'Is so it go sometimes. Just accept it, Agatha. That is how things go. Just accept it.'

It took hours before the last of her rage finally left her. She exhaled it in a heavy breath. She turned her attention to the child that was still attached to its dead mother. Agatha went over and held the baby, at a distance at first, but then she brought the child closer, and then closer still. She wiped the stale tears from her own wrinkled face.

'Sshhhhhhh,' she whispered, and made an effort to smile. 'Well, well, my dear. Maybe you is the child I was never able to have. And if I did have a little girl-pickney like you, I would have named her Adamine.'

So Agatha rocked Adamine in her arms, cooing to her. 'OK, my dear. OK. Mother Lazarus will make you a deal. Fifteen years I will give to you. Yes indeedy. Fifteen years, but not a day more.'

And the swarm of insects that had been fluttering in Mother Lazarus's fingers and her arms and her eyelids and her feet all flew away at once – like fireflies that lose their light and disappear with the morning.

an instalment of a testimony spoken to the wind

Shhhhhhhhh

IS LIE. THE Monsignor never come back quiet. He come back with vexation brewing in his heart, bubbling up like a pot of peas, and when he open the door and see what was before him, is like the lid of that pot explode. No sah. He never come back old. He get old because of what Miss Lily did do him. Listen, Mother Lazarus say even she who don't custom to fraid of nobody was fraid of him that day when he step back inside the house. Monsignor Dennis come back to see something that look like celebration, something that look like carnival or Jonkoonoo. People did wrap up in all kind of colours, everybody looking as bright as birds – Maas Paul with his blue bandages, Maas Johnson with yellow round his left foot and red round his right, Maas Johnny with orange on his body and on top him head. But most splendocious of all was Miss Lily. From her eyeball straight down to her toenail, Miss Lily was draped in purple. She was wearing bandage on parts of her body that never even need bandage. Monsignor Dennis wasn't pleased. Him shout out, *Miss Lazarus! Miss Lazarus!* Mother Lazarus right there beside him but she fraid to answer. He turn on her. *Explain this to me. Explain this, you silly old woman.* She don't answer him in her usual way for even she admit that sometimes she talk to him as if him was a boy. Not today. Instead she thinking to herself, *a soft answer turneth away wrath,* but though she know the principle, she can't think of the soft answer to give. *Missa Dennis, sir, I really don't see the harm . . . He throw his head back and laugh so loud it cut her off. Everybody surprise because nobody ever hear him laugh before. But there was no* joy in that laugh, and soon as it did start is as soon as it did stop. You do not see the harm? You do not see the harm? Of course, my dear lady, you are too bloody old to see anything. Well, you just take them off this instant. This very instant. Him was serious and before Mother Lazarus could say yea or nay, he bend down himself and start to tear off bandage like how a pickney would tear shine-paper off of a present. The whole time he was muttering bout the properties of dye, bout ink that if you don't mind sharp could seep into wounds, bout infection of the bloodstream. But he whispering it all to himself, like this knowledge was too much to share with the people who it really concern.

Shhhhhhhhh

All this time something terrible and strong was rising up in Maas Paul and in Maas Johnson and in Maas Johnny. But most especially it was rising up in Miss Lily. She was sick and tired of this man treating her like she was nothing more than a ball of donkey shit. He tear off the bandages from Maas Paul. He tear off the bandages from Maas Johnson. He tear off the bandages from Maas Johnny. But when he go to Miss Lily she lean forward in her chair and *kashai!* she thump him in his face. One almighty thump like she did have yam and dasheen and cassava in her fist. Have mercy! He never expect it. Never see it coming at all, at all, and he howl out. Listen nuh, any time they tell me this part of the story they all laugh and laugh just to think of Monsignor Dennis rubbing his face and looking so frighten. They say he jump up to his feet and bawl out, *What the devil has gotten into you lot of monkeys?* Yes, that's what he call them to their faces. Miss Lily push herself as far up in her wheelchair as she could go. She

63

looking like a man who just step out of the rum-bar and is suddenly unbalanced by the night air. She rocking back and forth but she looking on him steady, so steady that him cannot look away from her. Miss Lily was a schoolteacher once upon a time and she draw for that same sharp voice that used to make pickney stand up straight and behave themselves. Miss Lily herself never once repeat this speech to me, but the other fellows repeat it for her. And maybe they add to it, and maybe they subtract, but she never correct them. So if don't go so, it nearly go so.

Shhhhhhhh

Look here, sir, Miss Lily start, I know you do not know what it is like to look in a mirror and see a face as ugly as mine. And even if you did have what I have, you would be white so you would still be able to make a way in this world. So since you don't know, I will tell you: I have seen a man eat his food and throw it back up just because he catch sight of me. And another time a whole set of children throw dog shit at me and bawl out leper, and then they run away and laugh. The men were nodding like it was church. Tell him, Lily, tell him. She continue. But I wasn't born looking like this, sir. There was a time when I was a schoolteacher. I have my diploma from Mico Teacher's College to prove it. Furthermore I was a pretty young thing, and a tall gentleman better looking than even you was courting me in those days. We was supposed to get married. But then all on a sudden this thing start happening to me. The three men agreed, Yes, yes. That's how it start. All on a sudden. Miss Lily was getting bolder, her voice rising and breaking at the same time, So I said to myself, Lily, you can't go to church and turn Mrs with this bad case of eczema. That is what I did think it was. So I wait for it to clear. It is twenty years now and I still waiting. The man leave me of course. *Who could blame him? And furthermore I lose my looks. Furthermore I lose my man. Furthermore I lose my teaching work. Furthermore I lose every Godalmighty thing a person can lose. So see here now, Monsignor Dennis, it is a long long time now that I don't feel good bout myself. But take a long look at this ugly woman before you.* Miss Lily spread her arms to show the heap of purple that was covering her body. *All of this is making me feel beautiful again. And no way josé you going to take this from me.* She finish by spitting on the floor. *You, sir, is nothing but a cantankerous stinking old john-crow.* The three men repeat this with feeling, *Yes, yes, a stinking old john-crow.*

Shhhhhhhhh

Is like the words hit him harder than the thump him get. Like maybe he couldn't handle the thought of people like that, lepers, standing up to him like they was somebody. So from that day he leave them alone. He don't say nothing. He don't business. And his age come upon him hard. When I did get to know him years after, he was just a shadow of a man – a senile old priest who sometimes seem even worse off than the lepers. I remember one day Mother Lazarus sigh a heavy sigh and march outside to him, like something was on her mind and she had to speak it even if he never have the ears to hear it. *You know how old I be? You know how old I be, Missa Dennis? I is one hundred and one years old. You can't count that. I supposed to be in the grave now, but I still doing work here because you is wutless. I still on my hands and knees. Is a crying shame.* Monsignor Dennis look up at her and then he smile and ask, *Nancy, is that you?* He did start to do that, call people by whichever name did come to him. Mother Lazarus put her hands on her kimbo and is like she find a joke in this. She start to laugh and she say. *Well there you have it. We is abandoned.*

Shhhhhhhhh

What people in Spanish Town never want to see, they had to suffer and see. Lepers with all their sores sitting on whichever street corner they could capture, their hands stretch out for the whole day, hoping that somebody would drop a coin or two into them. More times people would just cross the road. I was lucky because I could walk up and down free and I never really have leprosy though I consider myself one of them. Sometimes if I see a woman who look to me like maybe she is a mother, I stop and ask her for money. Sometimes that woman turn round and ask why I not in school. I don't tell her that I can read and write, thank you very much, probably better than her own dunce pickney. In the same way when I reach this country, the nurses in the hospital always asking if I want them to read to me. I don't tell none of them how Miss Lily would sit me down every evening and learn me my lessons, and how I did read her favourite book plenty times and could recite chapter and verse from *Jane Eyre* without even look at the page. I don't bother to ask none of them the greater question – what good is writing and reading; what good is books when all the books in the world don't change the fact that some of us is born under a stone, and every try that we try to rise, we ongly buck our heads. The chaulmoogra oil did stop coming. The leprosy start to get worser and worser. Who never lose toes and fingers before, start to lose them now. Who did want to cry couldn't cry, because their tear ducts mash up. The house start to really fall apart.

66

The paint strip completely and you could no longer look on that house and think of anything soft; just plain hardness staring right back at you. The roof start to fall in and the garden get so overgrown it begin to look like wilderness. Sometimes when people pass, we hear them say, *Look pon that abandoned house*. I would think, but of course. It is an abandoned house for abandoned people. And I did know even then that that house was like my life. I know in my heart that I was destined for ruin. I know my life was going to be one big wilderness, full of chaff and stone, and this never cause no vexation in my spirit. I just accept it. That is what life was supposed to be. I was a leper. I consider all these things and I take them and call it as fact.

Shhhhhhhhh

One morning when it was coming on to my fifteenth birthday, I wake up and all around me was work. Like Sunday morning work when everything smell of polish and sugar, and every corner in the house shining like it new. Mother Lazarus was grating sweet potato, grating nutmeg, grating coconuts. I notice bowls of sugar and flour and cornmeal already measured out. I know this mean dukkunnu, and sweet potato pudding, and toto, and grater cake. But I was confuse. I ask her, *what all of this for?* She smile at me and say, *Suppose I tell you that all of this is for you? Yes indeedy. Tomorrow is the day of your womanhood, and we has to celebrate it proper.* Everybody else was doing their own bit of work, and each of them come over and hold my hand and shake it every time I pass them, and say, *you is not a little girl no more. Tomorrow you will come into your womanhood.* I start feel scared. I too shame to ask them what is this womanhood exactly? What will it look like? What will it do? I did think womanhood was when you start to bleed from your woman-parts, but it was four years since I was doing that. And I think womanhood was when your titty start to swell up, but my titties was already firm and did look like two big grapefruits in front of me and men would make rude talk when I pass, so I think, wasn't that womanhood? And if none of that was, then I scared to think what else going to happen to me tomorrow. I remember a story Mother Lazarus used to tell me:

Once upon a time a young woman wake up with nothing inside her. Like if you did look inside her eyes you would see that no thoughts was left inside her brain, that they all had been scattered. I trying to say that when this woman wake up, she was mad as shad. But when there is nothing inside you, you become hungry for what is missing. So she get up and start to walk, and she walk, and she walk, and she walk till she walk all the way to the dungle heap. When she reach the dungle she throw herself on the ground and start to dig. She don't have no shovel or no fork. Just her fingernails. And she dig, and she dig, filling up her fingernails with stone and pushing her own self deeper and deeper into the ground. Even the dogs and pigs did feel sorry for her and one of them ask, Lady, what is it you looking for? She never answer, but she didn't need to, for every creature know that when a woman can't find part of herself, then it loss inside the dungle heap. So the pigs and the dogs just look on with sadness. It wasn't no little bit of time that she was there digging neither, going deeper down into her own hole. She drink rainwater and she eat dirt. Moons did come and go, and the world did turn round, and is then at last that she finally find what she was looking for. A little pouch with her name write on it. When she open

68

the pouch black pepper and dirt fall out, and the same time all of her thoughts come back. She had undone the evil that had been done against her. But when time she look up, she see a wall that was as tall as a year. There was no coming out of this hole. She spend all that time digging what she couldn't escape from. Take warning, Adamine, that woman is still there today.

Shhhhhhhhh

That night when all the work done, and the food sitting down to cool, Mother Lazarus put on a fresh nightgown. She make me sit outside with her for a long time while she just mumble things to the sky. I know that Mother Lazarus was an old woman, but she never seemed so old to me until that night. I see that the skin under her neck was loose, and her lips was wrinkled. Finally she get up and she squeeze my hand and say, It is your turn now, Adamine. You is a woman now. It is time. And easy like that, she went to her bed.

Shhhhhhhhh

I find out that death comes to us like a flattening. For if your face had lines in it before, if it did rise up in certain places, all that gone once you is dead. You face will fall like a piece of paper, flat and blank. Nobody else did cry when they wake up to see that Mother Lazarus was gone. Me alone was holding her hand and bawling my eyes out. Miss Lily wheel her way into the room and did not even look at the body. She ongly look at me, like this was something she knew was going to happen for a long time. Happy birthday, is what she say. You is a woman now, and you is in charge. But I never want it to be my birthday.

69

I never want to be no woman. I never want to be in charge of nobody.

Shhhhhhhhh

That night I dream they was each calling out to me. Calling me, calling me every second. I dream that I could get no portion of quiet or peace. Not a minute to feel the breeze or to just sit back and watch Anansi Spider walking cross his web. Miss Lily and Maas Paul, Maas Johnny and Maas Johnson and even Monsignor Dennis was all calling me to come quick, come quick. Come and watch us dead. Come and watch the flattening come upon us. I couldn't sleep. Every time I close my eyes I hear my name: *Adamine! Adamine!* And for a week it was like this. So finally one night I jump out of bed. The air was cold. I run out into the yard and start to shout, *go to hell! Go to hell! Go to hell every last one of you!* They all wake up same time and come out looking so frighten. Miss Lily ask me, *what is wrong, child?* But I was still hearing the voice calling me so I get vex and I tell them some ten-shilling words. Still the voice never stop. *Adamine!* And then it say something else: *Lay down your burdens and follow me.* I press myself into a corner of the house and start to shiver, for I understand at last that this voice don't belong to nobody I know. It was the voice of the Lord, and it continue calling and calling till I make up my mind to follow.

Shhhhhhhhh

Wherever you is hearing this now, please don't make up your face as if to say I done a heartless thing. For it is written: if a man leaveth not his father and mother then

70

how shall he inherit the Kingdom? And it is written: no man, having put his hand to the plough, and looking back, is fit for the kingdom of God. And the Master himself told us plain, let the dead bury the dead. So I leave them there.

Shhhhhhhhh

I wasn't heartless, for when I hear what happened after, I grieve a terrible grieving. If I could wear ash on my head, I would wear ash on my head even now. If I had crocus bags to wear on my body, I would wear crocus bags on my body now. If I could rend my garments in two I would rend my garments in two, and in three, and in four, and in five. The newspaper did tell the story. Mr Mac drive up one day to check on things and smell something awful. He find Miss Lily sitting there in her wheelchair, her eyes wide open. He say he think she was barely alive when he find her, but I think his mind was playing tricks and even then she was dead. She was sitting mongst the corpses of the other men and flies was walking on their eyes and laying maggots in their sores. Monsignor Dennis was dead in the backyard. For days and days people was writing letters to newspapers and they say how it was a shame and a disgrace that these people was abandoned, and that people was people whether they be sick or not. Half of me feel shame, but the next half was angry, for I think to myself they was abandoned so long they didn't even know what it was to be considered. Everyone finding it easy to consider the lepers now that they was dead. People even begin to demand autopsy. They want to find out exactly what happened in those last days, what disease, or what autoclapse it was that hit them. Well, if they did the autopsy I never hear the results, but what I think is this: that it come a time when people who been sick their whole lives just get tired of being sick, tired of waiting to die, and they just say chu, and they give up. Simple as that. The family who grow me give up because I leave them. In the end it was me who abandon them. O Mighty God of Daniel, forgive me. They say you must talk the truth and shame the devil. So here is the truth: maybe some of the things that this Writer Man has put down on his paper is true after all. Like maybe he find out things I been trying to forget my whole life. Like, once upon a time there was a leper colony in Jamaica. But such a time is only once, and no more.

The Photo of the Warner Woman

You have come across a picture of Adamine, cut it from an edition of *The Jamaica Star*. It is a grainy black and white photograph of a twenty-five-year-old woman. Her face is blurred in this picture, the flash of the camera seeming to distort rather than bring it out. She is standing behind a table, so is only visible from the waist up. The table is not elaborately spread — just a basin of water at its centre. Behind her is the wall of the church in which the woman had risen to the position of Junior Mother. There are planks of board, and what appear to be two banners hanging on either side of her. On one of the banners a moon and star are the only things discernible. There is also writing on it, but this cannot be deciphered. The second banner is of such a dark shade that nothing beyond its general shape is clear. The woman is holding up a Bible, and while the flash of the camera distorts her face, it magnificently highlights her teeth — white and square, and so many of them.

You have thumb-tacked this picture to your door, hoping that when she passes it, Adamine, the Warner Woman, will catch a sudden glimpse of herself, that the past will all come rushing back to her. You have been playing this game for a while — tempting her memory to come back. Paintings of Revival in your flat, this one early picture of Adamine, and also you make sure to print out parts of the story, hoping she will read these bits

73

and maybe disagrees; hoping that things will come back to her.

But of course, what you really want is that one day she might remember you.

Part Two

IN WHICH THE STORY PREPARES TO TRAVEL,
AND THEN BEGINS AGAIN

an instalment of a testimony spoken to the wind

Shhhhhhhhh

SOMETIMES I TIRED of talking to this Writer Man. If I had my wish right now I would ongly talk to you. I would ongly talk to you because at least you hear me. I have said to Mr Writer Man, it don't take no great skill to write down a story. All you have to do is put one word after the next and you continue like that until it done. But it take a special skill to hear a story – to incline your ears towards what may seem like silence. For nothing in this world is silent, you just have to learn how to hear. And I would ongly talk to you because I cannot see your face. I can neither see it frown nor smile. And because I do not know what shape your face has become, I do not have to change the shape of my words to suit you. So maybe you is there smiling. Or maybe you is there frowning. Or maybe your face has become a wide land of bepuzzlement. I do not know. You hear me like how Miss Lily hear Miss Charlotte Brontë. Miss Brontë done dead and buried, but when Miss Lily read *Jane Eyre*, she hear the voice coming to her as if from a great distance. That is how you hear me. And if I had my wish, I would ongly talk to you for a next reason. See, I have come to like this hour of talking, this darkest hour of night when life done forget itself. The world is as quiet as the grave right now, like it making space for a story it has never heard. I come out on this balcony, always at this time, and I go back in when the sky begin to change colour. When I go back to bed, is like I barely put my head on my pillow and fall asleep when Mr Writer Man start to shake me awake again. *Top o' the morning*, he say, top o'

78

the morning. He have manners, I admit. He always make me a cup of tea. He know by now that I start my mornings with green tea and not the bitter coffee he make for himself. The first time I refuse the coffee he come to tell me like he proud, *but it's Blue Mountain coffee. It's from Jamaica.* I tell him that's all well and good, but it wouldn't make a goddam difference if it did come straight from my mama's titty. We take our cups and sit down. He turn on a little black tape-recorder and ask, *Are you ready to begin again, Adamine?* I don't think I is ever ready to begin again. Sometimes I get worried because I don't know what it is he want to know. I don't know what is the point of all this talking and taping and writing. Instead of beginning straight away, sometimes I let my eyes wander round the room. This living room is full of red, like it was made to be a warning unto duppies: stay far! The couch, the rug, the flower vases — all red. And on the wall across from where I sit there is a painting. You can tell Mr Writer Man is very proud of owning it. Once upon a time I used to think paintings was only of flowers, or bowls of fruit, or loose white women with just a little piece of shawl covering their woman-parts. But this painting is nothing like that. It is a painting of black women, and they is all wearing dresses, the colours as bright as the Garden of Eden. The woman in front have on a red dress of course. The one right behind her have on a green dress, and a next one have on yellow. The women are all tilting their heads way back, and their necks is as long as from here to tomorrow. It is a painting of black women, but when you see the group of them you think of queens or empresses. The first day when I reach here, I just stand up and look on this painting. Mr Writer Man come up behind me and I hear him say, *Yes. I knew you'd like this. Do you recognise it?* I tell him no sah, I don't know nothing bout art. *No, he say, I meant do you recognise what's going on — the ceremony, these women? Don't you see it's Revival. Isn't this what you were once a part of?* I just say Oh, and keep silent. I wonder how he expect me to recognise women who have a portion of night where they supposed to have noses and eyes and faces. You cannot tell one woman different from another. You couldn't say if one woman was maybe Bishopess Herbert or if another was Eliza, or if another was Sharon or Erna or Marcia. I have known Revival women, and I known the houses they lived in, and the men they did sleep with. But I don't know the women in this painting. All I recognise is that these women supposed to be like me, but I think the whole thing too pretty. And then an understanding come to me: this is what Revival is for Mr Writer Man. Something pretty. Something red and green and yellow that you can put up on your wall as decoration. I see how he smile at this painting and I see now that he don't know plenty things.

Shhhhhhhhh

He don't guess how Captain Lucas could sometimes take his long stick and beat the daylights out of you if he get a vision that you have sin in your life. And when Captain beat you, you can't say nothing. I get my first beating within the first month of joining the band. I did wake up one night and Captain Lucas was standing tall, tall in the doorway. He don't have on his headtie or his robe or his shirt or his trousers or nothing at all. His man-parts was standing tall and straight like him own self. Bishopess Herbert who did usually sleep beside me was nowhere.

I don't know where she gone all on a sudden. And truth be told, it make me excited that I am about to do big-woman things and that my childhood was now far behind me. When he put his man-parts up inside my body I bear the pain and try to move in a way that would please him. I try to make sounds that I imagine is big-woman sounds. But maybe I should have been quiet. Maybe he think I was taking too much joy from it. He never say nothing then, but when we was gathered at church the next night, waiting for him to deliver his sermon, I ongly feel when his rod bust open my head. He shout out Jezebel. He say God give him a vision that I was a Jezebel woman with Jezebel thoughts and Jezebel ways. I take the beating, meek as a lamb, and later that night I rub aloe on the places where the rod did break my skin. But Mr Writer Man don't know none of that. He think Revival is something simple, something beautiful to look at from afar. But Revival was pain and joy mix up together like flour and water. This painting real pretty for true. But when time I look on it, I don't see myself. I don't see any kind of life I ever live. I cannot put my nose against it and smell the night, or the almonds, or the sweat of eighty-five men and women. I cannot run my fingers along it and feel the small stones we did fall upon. I don't even see the colours of the frocks we did wear. Our frocks did have to wash and wear, wash and wear, a hundred times and more, till they was a shade as dull as dusk, duller than any colour in this painting.

O Zion Hear These Words

It is a well known fact in Jamaica that several men and women born between 1920 and 1960 were saddled with names their parents never intended them to have. In almost every instance this was the postmistress's mistake. For if a child was born at home, the parents could simply go to the post office and fill out a form. If they were illiterate, or just could not be bothered, they would have the postmistress fill it out for them. This led to all kinds of misnamings. Sometimes the postmistress simply heard wrong. At other times, out of spite or boredom, she decided to spell the name exactly as the parents had pronounced it. There is, for this reason, a whole generation of people in Jamaica who have H's in their names where there should have been no H: Handrew, Hanthia, Hantoinette, Hemily, Harnold. But the mistake made in the case of Adamine Bustamante was not because the postmistress did not hear the right name but rather that she wrote it down in the wrong place. The mother's name, Pearline Portious, was entered in the box which clearly said, Child's Name. And because, after being registered at the post office, a child might not need to see the birth certificate for years, many people went around not knowing what their actual names were. Adamine only found out hers when she was thirty years old and needed her birth certificate because she was about to come to England. She went to the Registrar's Office at midday. The sky was full of the sun, and a line of over three hundred people was slowly inching towards the counter. Most had stood there for many hours, the sun beating down on them and causing rivers of perspiration to pour from their bodies. When Adamine reached the queue, however, someone whispered, 'Warner Woman.' The crowd parted with a murmur and allowed her immediate access to the counter. A supervisor was overheard saying to a young clerk, 'You go deal with that one there. And deal with her good. I don't want she to call down no flood and storm on this office today!'

The young man approached Adamine with a slight tremble. 'Good morning, Mother.'

'I come here for my birth paper. I name Adamine Bustamante.'

'Yes, Mother,' the man said genuflecting and then disappeared. For the better part of an hour he searched and searched in vain. When at first he didn't find 'Adamine Bustamante' he suspected she might have been registered as Hadamine, but he didn't find that name either. He then suspected what was another common mistake, that her first name might have been entered as her surname, and her surname as her first. But that too produced no results. Finally he returned to the counter.

'Mother, I can't find the birth paper. Can you give me your date of birth and the parish where you was born?' Adamine gave him the information and he went off again, emerging at long last with the certificate in his hand.

'Mother,' he said, 'I think I find your papers, but I have to inform you, your name is Pearline Portious.'

The Warner Woman would tell you, however, that although man might have registered her name in one book as one thing, God had registered her name as another. And the name he knew her by was Adamine Bustamante. She knew this because this was the name she heard being called one night after Mother Lazarus had died, when she woke up suddenly, stepped out of the gate of the leper colony, and into another life. She had climbed the hill and trekked four and a quarter miles, arriving at a church which met under the broad sky, and where she started singing a song which actually had no words.

The group of eighty-four Revivalists – mainly women – who met every Monday, Tuesday and Wednesday night in Wariboka Vale, St Catherine, under the leadership of Captain Lucas Gilles and Bishopess Cynthia Herbert, and who called themselves the Band of the Seventh Fire, did not mean to have their meetings in secret. And yet, their meeting place was so far out of the way, across so many fields and stones and trees, it was generally accepted that anyone who managed to make it there safely, and in the middle of the night, and without a guide or an invitation or a moon to light the way, could only have been called and led by the Spirit. So on the night fifteen-year-old Adamine walked out of her childhood, and stepped from the trees into that clearing, and began walking towards this band of Revivalists, not one of them stopped dancing or singing or even looked on her too closely. They simply made room for her to join the circle.

Adamine arrived when the service had reached fever pitch, but it had begun hours earlier, as the final orange of evening faded and coconut and breadfruit trees lost their substance, becoming only silhouettes. The band members stepped into the clearing one by one, with a long, elegant walk that did not even know it was long and elegant, a song tumbling from their lips into the open space.

> There is a meeting here tonight
> There is a meeting here tonight
> Come one and all and gather round
> There is a meeting here tonight

Two brothers carried a bare table to the centre of the circle, holding it gently as if it were the Ark of the Covenant. Once it was put down, a sister spread the table with a fold of lace, and everyone placed what they had brought on it: oranges, star apples, bread, cakes, cream soda, candles. Then they laid out basins of water. Everyone bowed deeply before the basins, then bowed deeply before each other, and said how good and how pleasant it was to gather together in the name of the Lord. This greeting and bowing went on for quite some time until the three junior Mothers – women with pencils stuck behind their ears, scissors swinging from ropes tied around their waists, and rulers tucked inside their belts – took up their stations.

If you have been to Jamaica and seen such a woman, this whole attire may have appeared to be nothing but a curious display of stationery, but then you might not have understood the use of the pencil to write down prophecies, the use of the pair of scissors to cut away bad spirits, and the use of the ruler to measure out the days allotted unto man.

Captain Lucas Gilles, a tall gentleman with a pointy white beard and skin as blue-black as the night, lifted his hands and said, 'Blessed.'

Everyone said 'Blessed love' back to him, and he said 'Peace and love' back to them.

Bishopess Herbert waddled up to the table. She closed her eyes and swayed a little. She tilted her head as far back as it would go and with a voice that managed to sound both like thunder and music, she said a single word, stretching it out, holding the note and the vibration, 'Yeaaaaaaaaa.'

People began to toss their heads from side to side. Others simply whispered, 'Sweet Lord.' and so the Bishopess made the sound again, holding the note and the vibration even longer, until a few people were jumping.

The Spirit was going to come tonight. Everyone could feel it.

Bishopess Herbert half rumbled, half sang, 'When the angel come Him shall trouble the water-oh-hooooooooo.'

Everyone found the last part of this note and sang it back to her in a counter-harmony, 'Oh Hoooooooo.'

'Hear now de word of your God. De daughter of Babylon is like a threshing-floor, is time to thresh her. De time of her harvest is come. And though Babylon hath crushed us, and made us into empty vessels, though Babylon hath swallowed us up like dragons, though Babylon hath cast us out, oh hoooooo ...'

'Oh hooooooo.'

'... de violence done to we and to our flesh shall be visited upon Babylon. For our God will make de springs dry. And Babylon shall become heaps, a dwelling-place for dragons, an astonishment, and a hissing without an inhabitant. Babylon's children shall roar together like lion, oooh hoooooooo.'

'Oh hooooo.'

'Them shall yell as lions whelp. And them shall sleep a deep sleep and never shall they wake! Zion children! Zion children! Hear these words, for them is de words of your God. Ooooh hooooo.'

'Amen.'

Every eye was now turned to Captain Lucas, whose own gaze was set somewhere beyond. 'Seven and seven and seven.' he whispered.

It was the smallest of sounds but it was heard by everyone, and when he nodded it was the smallest of movements, but this too was seen and noted by all. The nod meant there was to be no sermon tonight, that the words from the Bishopess had been enough. So the drums came out, as if from nowhere, as if the night had been the cupboard in which they had been stored, and the same rough farm hands that had previously held the table as if it were the Ark now began to fall like sweet rain on the goatskin drums. And whoever was still feeling uptight, the music unlocked their mid-sections and a gentle rocking began. The first song rose.

Any-anywhere that the army go
Any-anywhere that the army go
Any-anywhere that the army go
Satan follow

Satan follow the army band
Satan follow the army band
Satan follow the army band
Satan follow

And if a Macedonia de army go
If a Macedonia de army go
If a Macedonia de army go
Satan follow

But Adamine had not arrived all those hours before. She had not seen them set the table, or heard the word, or the first song, nor the twenty that followed. She arrived only after they had exhausted all the words which could have been spoken, after they had exhausted all the lyrics which could have been sung, after the songs themselves had exhausted all the oxygen in that clearing, after the night had swallowed all its stars, and the sky had swallowed all its owls, and all that was left was an electric hollow, a magic space. Try as you might, you could not remain unmoved by it; nothing could stop the hairs on the back of your neck from rising. It was a space inside which even pigs and dogs were known to fall, slain by the Spirit. The Revivalists began to sing a song that had no words, just a heavy rhythmic breathing, a trumping, a *Hi wah hi, Hi wah hi!* a *Hm! Hm! Hm!* And it was in this moment that Adamine arrived. She was possessed immediately. She walked towards the group in a slow sideways shuffle, her head flung back and her hands dangling loosely behind her. Her chest, however, was rigid, thrust forward, and her hips gently undulated as she did her sideways movement towards the group.

No two Revivalists will describe possession in the same way. For one might call it a riding – you the horse, and the Spirit the jockey – another will call it a travelling. Another will say it is a tearing and freeing of soul from flesh. Adamine would say it wasn't a separation at all, merely a diminishing of your own body. She would tell you that she was always in her body, but the body felt smaller, less significant, as if she could now survive without food or water, and she understood then how people could go for forty days and forty nights in a wilderness and come back exalted. She understood that her body was not her, it wasn't even a part of her, because she would not be any less or any more if that body gained or lost weight, if it grew a tumour or lost a foot. Another Revivalist might describe possession as a kind of flying, a floating above the treetops. Adamine would not agree with this. Not completely. She would tell you it is your vision that becomes detached and can suddenly place itself anywhere. Vision, Adamine will tell you, is the gift of the possessed. She says it like this, 'When I fall to the Spirit, I see and I see and I don't stop seeing.'

On the night that she became the eighty-fifth member of the Band of the Seventh Fire, this is what Adamine Bustamante saw ...

Everyone was dancing in one way or another: some were rooted like chickens to a single patch of dirt, their hands clasped behind their backs, bringing one foot forward and then back; others were spinning, as if in the midst of their own tornadoes, their skirts fanning out like a sudden bloom of cereus; a few had fallen, and Adamine watched the three Mothers walking around to close the skirts of those who had fallen with the legs spread open; she also saw herself shuffling behind a group of twelve who had decided to march around the clearing seven times, dull machetes raised above their heads.

Then she saw a woman who wasn't dancing at all, who sat in the middle and knitted. Adamine had seen this woman once before in a picture. It was the Original Pearline Portious. Adamine blinked and then she saw Mother Lazarus. She blinked again and now she could see a whole congregation of men and women who sat or stood between the dancing Revivalists, floating in the air, a congestion of familiar spirits, each attached in some way to the dancers who were crammed into the clearing.

Adamine saw and she saw and she didn't stop seeing.

She threw her vision above the clearing and saw the many humps of dark hills rolling all the way to the Caribbean Sea; she could see patoos flying below her, the spread of their white wings, their big eyes scanning the ground for rats; she could see a few lights burning in shacks, and she could also see inside the shacks themselves: a man who was no more than fifty lay in his bed shitting himself, his eyes permanently trained to one corner of the ceiling. Two young women entered the room. One frowned. 'Lawd God. Him messing up himself again, and I just change him a hour ago.'

The other one, 'It rough to see him come to this. Last year this time he was still up and hearty, wasn't that so?'

'Yes, yes.'

'And he still not saying nothing?'

'Not a sound he make except the heavy breathing you hear him with now.'

In another house, everyone was sleeping, except a grey cat in the kitchen, which was trying to paw the cover away from a pot of stew peas.

At another house a young girl rested her chin on the edge of a bed and watched the sleeping figure of a boy about her age who coughed in his sleep.

At another house an old woman walked the perimeter of the yard, a smile creasing her eyes as she sprinkled black powder around the house. At the same time, in the bedroom, another old woman was watching from behind a curtain, a smile also creasing her eyes, before she sprinkled olive oil around the circle of her bed.

At another house Adamine saw two men. She thought they were

90

twins, but then realised it was the same man standing beside himself. One self was in a rocking chair but the chair was not rocking. A pipe lay on the floor, the tobacco spilled out. The second self was standing, looking at the version of himself that was still in the chair. Then he looked up into Adamine's eyes and said, 'I never expect to leave like this.'

Adamine saw and she saw and she couldn't stop seeing.

Her vision went out across a wet expanse of black, the sea which at this late hour had become a part of the sky, but without stars. Her vision stung from all the salt and so returned to land. It saw a tree heavy with red Julie mangoes and parrots sleeping in its branches. Adamine's vision travelled up a river. It saw a woman with scales for skin, and a fishtail for legs, whose hair was not so long as everyone kept saying, but tall and majestic like Mother Lazarus. It was River Mumma of course, and she sat on a rock, her belly fat folding over on to her scales. River Mumma looked up and smiled at Adamine, and Adamine knew that the smile was a blessing. She now saw ground spirits, fallen angels, pickney duppies at the top of coconut trees, trying with their spirit hands to shake the fruit free. Then Adamine was back at the clearing and she could see that she herself had now become one of the fallen women herself, her legs spread wide, and that a Mother had closed her skirt for decency's sake.

Adamine saw and she saw and she couldn't stop seeing.

And then her face was being wetted, and her eyes opened suddenly, and it was the daylight of a day she did not even know, and her head was in the Bishopess's lap, and the Bishopess did not look half so stern as she had on the night when she had been reading the scripture. There were no drums or people dancing or any table set with fruit. It was a whole other day. Adamine tried to shake the grogginess from her eyes. She realised now that Bishopess Herbert was whispering gently, almost a song, *Come back, Ada, come back ya.*

an instalment of a testimony spoken to the wind

Shhhhhhhhh

SOMETIMES THIS WRITER Man take five different stories and make them into one. Sometimes the things he put down not untrue, but they never happen in that order. The first time I go to the Revival Church they was meeting in the balmyard, not in no forest. And that was the night they send me to Mother Herbert who had been calling unto me. But there came another day when I did fall in the Spirit, and for true, I did stay fallen for days. So let me tell you what it was like: I did see ancestors, ground spirits, fallen angels, archangels. I see River Mumma sitting on her rock. I see Baby Duppy wrestling with coconuts, Injan Duppy jangling her bangles, Rolling Calf shaking him chains. I see a future of earthquakes. I see the past that is a haunting unto man. I go down to river-bottom and I see alligators, and I go up to the sky and I see a line of crows. Maybe you shake your head, but let me learn you a lesson right now: plenty knowledge is in this world. Enough knowledge that you can pick and refuse. And if you want, you can refuse to know plenty things, don't care how true those things be. I know things you does not know, and things you will never know. And it is sake of that – sake of this knowledge – that people have looked on me and called me old fool or crazy. They treat me like I is retarded. Imagine that. I is the idiot because I know what they don't know. Donkey say the world nuh level, and the world not level for true. Plenty knowledge is all bout you, but ongly some knowledge you will accept. So I learn to keep things in my breast. Telling it and shouting it not going to make no goddam

94

difference to anything or anybody. I understand how this life go. Whatever white man believe in with all his heart – that thing name religion; whatever black woman believe in, that name superstition. What white man go to on Sunday, that thing name church; but what black woman go to name cult. What white man worship is The Living God himself; but what black woman worship name Satan or Beelzebub. Whatever it is that white man accept in his heart is a thing that make all the sense in the world; but what black woman accept in her heart is stupidness and don't worth a farthing. Sake of what black woman know in her heart, sake of her knowledge, she will get thrown into the madhouse and she will feel the pain of electric shock. So sometimes is best she keep silent. After all, don't care how you want to sit there and deny the knowledge of River Mumma sitting on her rock; don't care how you deny the knowledge of fallen angels who can jump into your body as they please; or the knowledge of ancestors who sit beside your bed and watch when they not harkening on to the sounds of drumming – don't care how you deny any of it, all of it still true. All of them things still exist, because them do not need the permission of your belief. But I talk these things careful and slow, cause I learn my lesson good. I taking time with my story. I know the value of silence. Sometimes silence can save you from being locked up. Sometimes silence is all that we have left.

Shhhhhhhhh

Mr Writer Man is not always a patient man. I telling him my story in its own way, in its own time. But some days is like he not listening. He looking off into the distance, through the windows and unto the snow. He tapping his pencil against the table like he not concerned with anything I saying. Irritation all over his voice when his mind finally come back to the room and he tell me to stop, stop . . . just hold on a minute. He flip the tape around in his recorder and before he press the buttons to start again, he ask me, *Adamine, please, we've been through all of this already. You're telling me the same things over and over. When are you going to tell me about England?* Well, well. I don't take talk like that from him. No sir. I set my voice firm as iron and tell him, *we will get there when we get there.* I tell him, *look all around you. England is now. But every now don't simply reach so by itself. Every now have its before. Every destination have its journey. The Apostle Paul did have to walk the Damascus Road, and the Saviour did have to walk up the steep hill of Calvary to get to his cross.* I tell him just like I will tell you now — *be patient, be patient. I wasn't always this old woman. I have a past that I need to sort through.* If he puff up his face when I say something like that, then I get up from the sofa and I say, *listen now, it was you who did come knocking on my door. I was contented and at peace living where I was living. The world did long ago forget bout me. But it was you who did take up your own self one evening and come asking for me.* I frown when I hear the name on your lips, *Pearline Portious,* because I tired of explaining that that is not my name. I ask you, *what is it that you want?* You ask me if I is the same Pearline Portious who . . . *and you pause for a short while . . . who was once at Saint Osmund Mental Hospital in Warwickshire.* I try to close the door on you. I wanted to slam it. I feel so fraid. I think you want to take me back to that place. But it was you who beg me please, please. You make big promise that you don't mean me no harm. You say you just need to ask some questions. So I let you come in and I let you say what you had to say at last. You walk in circles and circles like you was walking the surface of the earth. You keep on stopping and looking towards me.

You finally say, I never had an idea of what you would look like, but I never imagined you would look like this. You reach to touch my face, and I move away. Who the hell was you to be familiar like that? And I still fraid. I cannot stop from nervous. I tell you to please talk whatever it is that you have to talk. So at last you say to me, Miss Portious, I have a strange proposal for you. I stop you. First thing's first, my name is Adamine. Adamine Bustamante, and that is my true true name. You will please to call me that. You lift your eyebrows high like you confuse, but you say, all right . . . Adamine, Adamine . . . like you testing my name in your mouth . . . well, that's a pretty name, isn't it? I don't answer you. I tired of white people talking down to me like they think I is a stupid pickney or something. You continue — Well, as I was saying, Adamine, I know you will find this strange, but I would like you to consider coming to live with me for a few months. I think I start to choke right then, but you was still talking — I have a comfortable place and an extra room all set up for you. You look at me and I see that you was serious. Your green eyes was waiting right then for an answer. So I start to laugh. I don't laugh so hard in years. Like I suddenly alive again. I thinking, maybe you is the man I used to dream bout who was supposed to come and take me out of every goddamned place they lock me up in. But you come too late. I wonder who you really is then . . . who is this young white man putting question to an old woman like me, as if he trying to court me? Who is this man who want to pull an old woman from her life? I laugh and then I laugh some more. But you never even crack a smile. You wring your hands round and round. I'm serious, Adamine! You say it sharp, I want you to come and stay in my flat . . . I want you to consider it. You see, I am a writer . . . Oho! I say, you is a Writer Man? Of books and all them things? Yes, you say. And, I need your help with the book I am writing now. It's about a Warner Woman. And this time I look at you serious. I never hear an English man talk bout 'warner woman' before. The words sound funny in your mouth, with your speaky-spokey accent. I get curious and sit down. Tell me more, Mr Writer Man, I say to you. Well, Adamine, all I would like is for you to talk. That's all really. Just talk to me, tell me about your life, and I will listen. I get real quiet then. One and two and three minutes pass us by in that silence. Neither me nor you saying a thing. I will tell you now what was going on in my head — I was thinking bout my life. I was thinking bout the sixty-two useless years of my life — this life that somebody was suddenly interested in. I look it over because that is what you do when somebody come and ask you to borrow a tablecloth or something. You look it over to make sure it is presentable. But see here, my life wasn't presentable at all. There was gaps everywhere. Big gaps like when the rain come down heavy and a piece of the road fall away, and you can never walk that way no more. That is what my life was — a whole bunch of wash-away roads, none of them leading nowhere. I wonder to myself, how I could lose so much life just like that? Where it just vanish gone? My life — like a ruined tablecloth that can't give out to nobody. You was waiting so patient, but I decide my mind and I tell you no. I say it simple and quiet and sure. No. And you said, Please, Adamine. I know it may seem strange ... My no became louder then. NO! Hear me now, Mr Writer Man, I sick and tired of sitting down and talking things that make people look on me funny. I is not no lunatic. I is not from Mars. I come from Jamaica. And that is just so, it don't need no explanation and it don't need no story. What the hell you want to know bout warning? All you want to know is that you can write down that I is a crazy mad smaddy. But hear this — plenty people beat you to that already! Plenty people done write down that I mad, and maybe they is right. You don't need my help or my permission. So go on bout your business and leave me in peace, Writer Man. My answer is no ... Then you reach out towards me, and is like I could feel you holding my hand and I never want to pull it away. Please. You was trembling, and you say please as many times as I could say no. You promise me you would be patient. You promise me I could tell you my story in my own time and in my own way. And I tell you the God's truth, that was the best

98

thing you could have said. It move me. I start thinking ... my own story, in my own time. My own story, in my own time. I thinking if I do that, maybe I can find the lost roads. I thinking, finally somebody will hear me out proper. I wanted to do it. I wanted to tell you everything I could. But always remember, it was you, Mr Writer Man. It was you that promised to be patient, to listen to my story in its own order. So why now that I doing just that, you have started to frown? Why now that I is here, in your house, telling you how it really happen, you have started to change up my words as if it was ever your story to change? And why the hell did you come looking for me in the first place? You take me out of a place where I was not troubling a goddam soul and you bring me to a place of bad memory and tribulation.

Shhhhhhhhh

When time I say all of that to him, I see like a sadness wash over his face. He sit up. He turn off the tape-recorder and start to wring his hands round and round, and walk in a circle like the first time I meet him. Finally he look up and he look me straight in the eye. Him lips start to tremble again. Him say his words slow slow, as if he want me to catch every one. Even now his words is like a haunting unto me. I don't understand their meaning. He say, You may not remember this, Adamine. It was twenty-five years ago. But the first time it was you who came looking for me.

The First Warning

Bishopess Herbert lived in a Jamaican tenement yard – an inner-city squashing together of people. At times it seemed the yard had even more people than mosquitoes of which it had the usual swarms, their buzzing, black bodies fatter than the children from which they sucked. There were six bedrooms. In these six bedrooms there lived four families. Between these twenty-two people, there was only one bathroom and one kitchen. The mathematics became difficult. On most days the yard felt like an oven, so despite the fact that before Adamine arrived the Bishopess had lived by herself and was the only resident of the yard to enjoy the luxury of a room that was all her own, it had still become her habit to pass the evenings sitting by the gate, a damp rag on her face and another on her enormous breasts. When Adamine moved in, effectively doubling the population and temperature of her single room, they both began to pass the evening in this fashion. Under the shade of her two rags, Bishopess Herbert instructed Adamine in the mysterious ways of God.

'Just as every donkey have him sankey, so too everybody have him own gift. And according to what gift each somebody have, that will determine what colour they wear. One man maybe get the gift of oils and baths and herb mixing, and so he will wear a white head wrap. One woman will have the gift of talking deep Africa talk, she will able to call on the ancestors, and so she will custom to wear blue. Still another person might have the gift of song, a next one the gift of miracle working, and so on and so forth. And they wear yellow or black or green according to what manifestation of gift they have inside them. But Adamine girl, women like you and me have the most specialest gift of all. We get the gift of warning.'

Adamine had never before considered herself the kind of person who was talented at something. She never thought she was destined to be anything. She thought her life was simply a matter of surviving each day, until the day she no longer could do that.

'Ada, you is the woman who will wrap her head in red.'

'Like you.'

'Yes. We both have the same gift. But still, we is the women who have the largest portion of grief in this world. Is we who band our belly and bawl tears for people whose eyes too dry and whose heart too hard. We is Warner Women. Plenty people fraid of we, but that is because they fraid of truth. We is daughters of Jonah and of Legba.'

'Who that?'

'I see you don't know nothing. Tonight you must read the Book of Jonah before you go sleep. Jonah was a Warner Man from Bible days. It was him who almost dead inside the belly of a whale. And I tell you what: the whale did swallow Jonah because Jonah did swallow the warning that God give unto him. Don't you ever make that mistake, Ada. Learn that now. Don't ever fail to utter the word that God giveth you to utter, for people have to consider the words of Jesus.'

'I know bout Jonah. Is the other name I never hear before.'

'Papa Legba. Not plenty people call him by that name here. But that's what he name. Legba. If he had a book it would be long from here to there. Is Legba who stand at the crossroads and speak the language of God and the language of man, and everybody understand him. Angel and demon and man. Legba come to us all the way from Africaland to speak message to we. Yes, learn that.'

102

Adamine nodded. It was a lot for her to take in. And then she was curious. 'So what warning feel like?'

'Every somebody who have the gift feel it different. One woman will tell you it feel like when time you have a baby up inside your belly, and your water break. Such a woman will tell you that warning is like the baby coming out fast fast. That is why some Warner Woman scream out loud. Another Warner will tell you she don't remember a thing when it come upon her. Her eyes will roll way back deep in her head and if she look on you, all you see is white. But is Legba who jump into her skin. That kind of woman won't know where she walk, or what she talk. When she come back to herself, all on a sudden, she find that she standing up in the middle of a strange road, and people all around is bawling their repentance unto God. To me, warning is like a heaviness in my mouth. It is like a stone on my tongue. It is like my tongue have a new balance and I don't know how to speak with it no longer. Those times I know it is best to just relax and let the spirits talk through me. But you, Ada, you will feel it in your own way.'

'But how you know I have the gift of warning then, Mother?'

Bishopess Herbert observed Adamine carefully and then shook her head. 'Because all day I been seeing the spirit of Legba all over you, child.'

'Yes.' Adamine nodded. 'I think I see him too. When I wake up this morning and look in the mirror, I see an old man right there on top my head. An old man with a leg twist up like him want to dance DinkiMini.'

The older woman was taken aback. In her experience a young convert took months, even a year, before they could see and identify their attending Spirit. But the girl had described Legba perfectly.

'Yes, daughter, that's him. The one and the same. Legba all over you, child. Him trying to whisper something to you. When time warning come, you don't need to listen to no weather man to know bout storm or breezeblow. You just feel it in your spirit. But

Legba been at your ears all day, and if you can see him, that mean it won't be hard to hear him. He trying to tell you something, Ada. Listen to him, mi child. Listen and warn.'

So Adamine inclined her ear towards the old man who floated above her head. The old man inclined his lips to her ear. He began to whisper and Adamine began to frown. Suddenly, her heart was tight in her chest.

'No,' she whispered.

'It always hard to hear the first time,' the Bishopess said serenely.

'Please, no.' Adamine trembled.

'Sometimes it will be like a burden on your spirit. But still, it is the highest of gifts. You is highly favoured to receive it, child.'

'No!' Adamine shouted.

'Yes,' Bishopess Herbert whispered, looking off into the distance. 'Whatever Legba say is true. Whatever he say, it always go so. Don't fight it.'

'Jesus Christ have mercy!' Adamine shot up and started running.

Bishopess Herbert shook her head slowly, watching the fleeing figure of the girl. 'Poor thing,' she muttered knowingly. 'It always hard the first time.'

✳

Adamine's heart felt like there was a cow trapped inside her ribcage, like it wanted to come out of her chest right then. Still, she kept on running. Her feet stamped panic into the ground. Gravel, concrete and grass bore the imprint of her distress. She wondered why it was called a warning if you couldn't stop it happening. She ran across the market. She cut across people's yards. Then at last she was running up into the green mountains behind Spanish Town. Four and a quarter miles she ran. She was skidding down a path as familiar to her as her own life. She saw the perimeter fence. She saw the gate that was always open. Then she saw Mr Mac running out from one of the bungalows. 'Help!' he was shouting, as if there was someone in those mountains who could hear him. 'Help, smaddy call the doctor, get the ambulance quick!' as if such things existed so far inside the island.

Adamine did not bother to step through the gate. Her prophecy pushed her down to her knees and she began to tear at her hair. Her scalp bled. She spread her arms wide, the tufts of hair like black cotton caught between her fingernails. She stood up then and began to spin furiously, she and Legba shouting together, 'Death Warrant! Death Warrant! Death Waaarraaannnttt!'

an instalment of a testimony spoken to the wind

Shhhhhhhhh

IF YOU ASK any school pickney what they want to be when they grow big, they maybe tell you doctor or lawyer or politician, or any number of topanaris jobs. But not a one of them would say they want to become a Warner, because they know that is the hardest job of all, and one that is full of persecution but not so full of pay. And besides, some things in life you can strive for, but other things you can ongly be called into it. And warning is a thing like that.

Shhhhhhhhh

The two most famous Warner Women from Jamaica was one that did name Bernicey, and another whose name was Maud. One morning in the year that was 1907 Bernicey tie her head and walk up and down Kings Street, and she bawl out, *A lion stretcheth forth his paws under the earth, and this lion roareth, and this lion prepareth himself to run underneath our feet. So repent, my people, before it get too late!* Same time Maud was walking up and down Parade, shouting out, *A dragon cometh from the sky to breathe a terrible breath of fire. He breathes a terrible breath of fire unto the city. Repent!* But nobody pay neither of them no mind. Everybody continue with their wickedness. So the lion and the dragon come for true. When the Great Earthquake rock the city that same evening, people would say, *is like a lion is running underneath the earth.* And when the earthquake did done and the fire start to burn, people would say, *is like a dragon come down from the sky to breathe a breath of fire unto us.* To this day no

108

one know quite how many did dead in that earthquake, but I know of two. Bernicey and Maud. Like their own warnings wasn't enough to save them. Their houses fall on top of them same way. And so tell me which pickney would want such a life, to always know what is on the other side of Now, to always hear the future coming on its unstoppable hooves, to wake up one night in a terrible sweat, knowing, *behold, the end approacheth!*

The Cry of the Warner Woman

The cry of the Warner Woman is Warrant. You may imagine her as a kind of police woman who has come from a country in the sky; who has spent her entire morning waiting in a dusty room. In this dusty room a ceiling fan makes revolutions as slow as the hand of a clock. The Warner Woman waits. Letters have been stencilled on to the door outside, and together they read: Bureau of the Affairs of Men. Angels in suits specially tailored to accommodate their wings are sitting behind oak desks. They have severe grey eyes and their balding heads have been polished bright, so bright they are often mistaken for haloes. The angels carefully read through thick books. The Warner Woman waits. The angels at last begin to write up warrants. The warrants are handed to the Warner Woman. She rides down to Earth on a silver cloud. The spinning of her head, wrapped in its red turban, is like a siren. The Warner Woman cries Warrant, and if you have ears to hear her cry, her warrant has been served.

The cry of the Warner Woman is Storm & Hurricane & Flood! You may imagine her rising from the ocean floor, her naked body encrusted in barnacles. And now she is standing on the water; the white froth of the waves is obedient to her and follows subtle instructions from her toes. The Warner Woman is like a vessel. She carries people inside her. A mother perhaps, and grandmothers, and great-grandmothers, generations of prophets inside her. But also she carries the drowned. A crew of drowned niggers who gave themselves over to salt, who have been patient, who have sat on the ocean floor and waited for their beautiful legs to rot down to bone so that they could step away from the balls of lead they were chained to. They have sat, as children might sit, in a classroom, and have mastered the movements of the tide, have learned how to control it and turn it into something terrible, something like vengeance. The Warner Woman's cry of Storm & Hurricane & Flood is also their cry. It is a conjuration of salt.

The cry of the Warner Woman is Earthquake. You may imagine her walking on tectonic plates. She shakes. She passes on her shivers. The Warner Woman causes tremors in the hearts of men. Her words can be measured on Richter scales. She says to you, 'You have been living on a fault-line. The fault-line has shifted. You are falling through it even now.'

The cry of the Warner Woman is Consider. She draws you into contemplation, saying, Consider that, and then consider this. Consider yourself, and your deeds. Consider the consequences of things. Consider the lilies of the field, how they grow; they toil not, neither do they spin. And yet I say unto you, even Solomon in all his glory was not arrayed like one of them. Consider the ant and be wise. And consider the ravens who neither sow nor reap nor have storehouses or barns, and yet the Father feedeth them. So consider yourself, and your place in the world, how ye are but a speck of dust.

The Warner Woman walks on normal roads. She travels on normal buses. Like everyone else, the Warner Woman must go out from her house to buy bread. She must get a cylinder of gas for her stove. She has a normal job. She works at the garment factory. Or she washes clothes. Or she is in your kitchen preparing your dinner. The Warner Woman looks like everyone else, but for the headpiece she occasionally wears. But for the rulers in her headpiece. But for the pencil stuck behind her ear. Most days as the Warner Woman walks on her normal roads, and travels on her normal buses, she keeps her own counsel. Like everyone else she must get through the day's trials. But when the Warner Woman cries out suddenly, her cry enters people's blood like a freezing. No longer is she just another woman on the road, or a woman on the bus. She has become the Warner Woman. The Terrible Warner Woman. Her whole body becomes rigid. She dips. She comes back up. When the Messenger Spirit is upon the Warner Woman you must look every which way but in her eyes, because in her eyes you will see Port Royal, you will see Kendal, you will see Kingston besieged by Cholera, you will see the single grave for one thousand men, you will see the fires and the hangings of 1861; you will see it all. You must make the sign of the cross while the Warner Woman spins, hoping the Warner Woman will say to herself – here is someone who has considered all that needs considering, someone who does not need further warning. When she bolts towards someone, you will hope it is not you, but if it is, you will have the respect to freeze on the spot and try not to mess yourself in public. The Warner Woman lays her hands on the forehead. Her cry is Warrant! Storm & Hurricane & Flood! Earthquake! And more terrible than any of these: *Ward 18! Ward 18! The Messenger Spirit just come tell me that it is Ward 18 for you!*

Of all the wards at the Public Hospital this was the most infamous. To doctors it was simply known as Ward 18 but to everyone else – nurses, patients, the general public – it was also known as Ward 'Lord me done!' So certain were Jamaicans of their impending death if admitted to this ward that relatives would start the grieving process immediately, calling family members from around the world, telling them to come back home for the funeral. In fact, many a moving Sunday morning testimony began, *Brethren, them did put me on Ward 'Lord me done!'* The congregation would gasp. *But the blessed Saviour never done with me at all!* To which the congregation would shout Amen.

The cry of the Warner Woman carries with it a scent, and if you

113

are close by when she prophesies you will smell it too. It is the smell of nutmeg, of earth, of rocks, of rain coming in from a distance, of salt, of ocean, of egrets, of oil, of cream soda, of coconut, of dust.

an instalment of a testimony spoken to the wind

Shhhhhhhhh

JUST AS EVERY fruit don't name mango, and just as every animal don't name dog, so too the Warner Woman's mouth is not only full of thunder and lightning. It is true, many times I did cry Warrant. And Flood. And Earthquake. But sometimes the cry of the Warner Woman is Peace. Peace and love I bring to you, Peace and love. One day I may tell you of the storm, but the next day I may tell you to cast your eyes to the east where there riseth a rainbow. And furthermore, sometimes a warning is not a thing to be avoided, nor a thing to fear. Like when I did first join the Band of the Seventh Fire, and the message of the Lord did come unto me saying, Beware, a thief cometh in the night. But lock not your doors, Ada. Close not your windows. For this thief is a man as tall and slender as the palm tree, and he wanteth only your heart and your love.

Shhhhhhhh

But warning was never easy with me. It was a thing more terrible than woman cramps. It feel like when you eat something bad and a sickness start to grow in your belly, and it grow and it grow until you just need to throw it up. That's what warning was – something that grow inside you and make you feel miserable till you spit it out. And I tell you what – I never know pain like the day when I decide to give it all up. I never just sick for days; I did sick for years. More years than I can bother to count. I thought I was going to dead. But in this country that

116

name England, things is different. Warning ongly going to get you in trouble here. Warning ongly going to make the nurse strap down your hands. Warning ongly going to get you the electric shock. Warning ongly going to cause you to have to sit before a bald-head doctor you never like from morning and now you have him staring at you for hours. Him is the expert, the know-it-all, but he want *you* to do the talking. When you don't talk Mr Doctor say you not co-operating. When you do talk, all you hear from him is *delusions* and *visions of grandeur* and *hallucination*. So this is where I come and find myself, between a rock and a rock. If I don't warn, I feel sick, but if I warn, I get in even worser trouble. So after a time I just keep silent and bear the pain. If I feel the need to spin, I don't spin. If I feel the need to shout, I don't shout. I stop completely. I just wait and wait for the day when the Father's word would stop rumbling in my belly-bottom and my tummy would finally settle. I cry and cry like spoil pickney who don't get his porridge. And in the nights when the lights turned out, I bawl like Elijah in his cave. I start to eat aspirin like how people eat food, and when that don't work, I beg for morphine. I say, God, if ever you did love me, make this cup pass from my lips. But still I continue to get warnings. Still I hear voices tormenting me. *Rise up, Daughter of Zion. Rise up Daughter of Jonah and Legba. I tell them no. I is ongly the daughter of Pearline Portious. I am ongly the girl who did born amongst the lepers. I never make for this.* And if you could do more than hear my voice, if you could also behold me, you would see a dried-up old woman. My ongly talent was that once upon a time I could warn. I could make people consider the words of their God. But I can't even do that no more.

The Fame of the Warner Woman

The cries of Adamine Bustamante were in fact so terrible and so often true, and the timbre of her voice which she threw into the wind so powerful, that her cries became famous. In the 15 July 1967 edition of the *Jamaica Star*, from which you have cut a picture of her, there is also a short article written by one Henry Kirkpatrick. It is quizzically titled 'The Last True Warner Woman?' and reads:

After the tragedy at St Catherine Gorge last Wednesday in which a bus full of high-school children overturned at Flat Bridge, many residents of Spanish Town are insisting the incident could have been prevented. While police continue to question the driver of the bus, who lost control of the vehicle as he attempted to cross Flat Bridge, many are insisting the tragedy was not only due to wet roads.

'Mother did tell them! She hold on to the bus before it leave and shout out, 'Waters rising and pickney drowning! Death Warrant!' What not clear in that message? People must learn to take warning,' insisted one woman who said she was on hand on Wednesday morning and witnessed the Warner Woman's prophecy.

The Star managed to catch up with the now famous Warner Woman, who was somewhat reluctant to give an interview.

'Whatever I do, I only do it for the Lord. I don't do it for fortune nor fame. When I get warning, I give it. Simple so. Plenty things in this world could prevent if people's ears never full up of wax. Everybody bawling bawling now for school pickney weh dead. But is plenty more warning I give, and nobody take heed.'

an instalment of a testimony spoken to the wind

Shhhhhhhh

IT NEVER NEED God to make people know that that bus was going to crash. The driver, a man by the name of Sam, did drive reckless from time. But when I see him that morning walking to the bus, I shake my head. His legs was already trembling and couldn't find a straight line, for him was the kind of man that sayeth unto himself, *what is life for but to drink wine and be drunk.* But the Lord say every thing in its season, and Sam was a man who never consider these words. On top of that, the set of pickney who was climbing on to the bus appear to me like some demons released straight from hell's furnace. They was making one heap of noise and talking nasty talk, like they wasn't nobody's children. I know something awful was going to happen so I try to stop it. I give them a warning. But may as well I did warn a stone. The bus drive off same way, and half-hour didn't pass before I get to understand it fall into the river. When the newspaper man talk to me and the article come out, it was like my name grow wings. Who never know me before suddenly know me. People was coming up to me and shaking my hand as if to say I was supposed to be proud. As if to say this crash was a thing that me did orchestrate. But who could be so heartless to feel proud that a set of pickney was dead? Them did need talking to, yes, and perhaps a good caning cross their behinds, but them never need to dead, and I take no joy in that. But people was talking talking like it was me who push the bus off the road with my own arms. One morning I even had to keep myself hid, because up and down the lane in St Jago, the father of

122

one of those dead children was walking. He was waving a gun, and looking for me and shouting, *weh she deh? Which part she deh? Bring out the stink bitch and see if God can save her from bullet!* Part of me did want to go out and stand up cool, cool before him and say, *Son of man, be cursed. Don't you dare threaten the Lord's anointed.* And believe you me I was brave enough to do it, for I consider to myself the words that did come to the prophet Jeremiah – for they shall fight against thee, but they shall not prevail. Still, I decide to stay hid, because I know it was just the grief inside that big man, making him carry on with his foolishness, and in truth, part of me was grieving right side with him.

Shhhhhhhhh

Well, who never want to kill me, all on a sudden want to be my friend. Shepherds and Captains of different bands was coming to me in secret, saying why I don't join their bands. They was promising to make me senior Mother of the church and all these kinds of things. I don't pay none of them no mind. I wasn't going to profit from dead pickney. I never pay no mind to the politician man either. He come knocking on my gate – a stout dark man with silver in his hair – and he ask me to stand with him on the platform whenever him was to give a speech. He tell me I don't have to do nothing more than just stand there, and maybe give a warning to the man from the party him was running gainst. This politician man look strange in his sharp black suit, standing up in the ghetto of St Jago, his big black car that could barely squeeze its way through the lane behind him. I consider my child-hood dreams, when I used to think that Father Bustamante would have did drive up in a car like that to fetch me.

But I just kiss my teeth and shut the gate on the politician. And people tell me I was a fool. They tell me I should not treat an MP like that. But understand this – I answer not to man; I answer only to the Most High. Besides, every season have its beginning and its end, and though my name was large for a time, it wasn't long before they forget all bout me.

The Balmyard

That Sunday had truly belonged to the sun. The round yellow beast had beat down so hard and had warmed up the zinc roof so much that underneath it felt like an incinerator. But Captain Lucas did not seem to have taken any notice, or if he had, he had decided to turn the experience into a song. He had asked the band of worshippers to sing it over and over,

> I wish somebody soul woulda ketch a fire
> Ketch a fire, Ketch a fire
> I wish somebody soul woulda ketch a fire
> Bu'n them with the Holy Ghost!

The service went on longer than usual. Three women fainted, and people were kind enough to assume this was because of the Spirit and not the stifling heat. But at last it ended and the skyjuice man who had dozed off just outside the balmyard was now rewarded as a flock of women jostled around his cart wanting to buy his cooling drinks of shaved ice and syrup. Adamine frowned. She listened to the women chattering excitedly, saw the glittering specks of shaved ice alight in the air, saw the exchange of money. Captain didn't like this sort of thing. He had told his congregation over and over, 'Don't turn the balmyard into a marketplace. People wouldn't be selling if you wasn't buying. Buy farther down the road.'

But all of this was forgotten on third Sundays, especially on days

125

like this when the sun had been beating down and the women had shouted and sung so much their mouths had become dry and swollen. On first and second and fourth Sundays the Band of the Seventh Fire met in different places – with other bands, on street corners, sometimes in the forest, or by the river – but third Sundays were special for they met at their own home, the seal ground, the balmyard. This was where Captain Lucas Gilles lived and it was in the middle of a St Jago slum. There was a trick to finding the balmyard, and people who did not know it could get lost in the maze of zinc and corrugated iron. The trick was simple: one had only to look to the red flag. The flag was mounted on a tall bamboo pole in the centre of the balmyard and once you entered the St Jago slum, it could be seen from almost anywhere. So although it would feel like you were walking in circles, if you fixed your eyes on the flag and simply walked, one foot in front of the other, eventually you would be guided safely into the sanctuary. Inside the balmyard there were many altars, simple wooden stands. On top of each stand was a container of water, and at the base was a cardboard sign with writing that appeared to be in Hebrew. There were three buildings, each standing right next to the other, each one dilapidated, a mismatch of scrap board and zinc. The first building was the room in which Lucas slept. The second was the broad shed into which the eighty-five members of the Band of the Seventh Fire would cram themselves. The third building was a fowl coop full of white chickens who squawked all day, but who, despite their racket, could never compete with the Band when they met for service.

Adamine was sitting on a concrete block in the yard and was watching as the women got their skyjuices and marched down the road together. Soon almost everyone was gone. Adamine felt a hand rest on her shoulder. She did not look up but reached up to pat the hand. 'I will stay around here for a little while longer, Bishopess,' Adamine said. 'You will be all right to get home by yourself?'

'Then I look so old that I wouldn't be all right?' Bishopess

Herbert chuckled, and then added in a lower, more conspiratorial tone, 'Well I glad to see you and the Captain getting on so good. You will reach far if you continue to sit by him feet. Plenty revelation come to Captain. Plenty.'

Adamine had been doing more than just sitting by the Captain's feet. She squeezed the older woman's hand. 'I will see you later then.'

'Yes, my child. Later. Don't hurry back.'

Adamine watched as Bishopess Herbert ambled to the gate. She frowned to see the Mother of the church also stop by the skyjuice vendor. Sipping on her drink, she continued up the road and disappeared. At last everyone was gone. Adamine got up from the concrete block and went over to shut the gate. The skyjuice vendor looked up as if expecting to make a final sale. Instead Adamine closed the gate with a slam.

'Fuck you too,' she heard him shout.

Briefly she considered opening the gate again, just to glare at him and have the satisfaction of watching him tremble, stealing from him what she knew would be his boast later on that evening to his friends, 'Those Revival people don't scare me none at all. I look at them and tell them fuck off, same so.'

But she resisted the temptation and walked instead into the first building where Captain Lucas was already disrobing. She sat on the edge of his bed.

'It was a powerful sermon today,' she said. 'Is like Archangel Gabriel was speaking mighty through you.'

The Captain nodded. 'Seven and seven and seven.' These were his own mystical words. He said them often and no one could agree what the incantation meant, or what it was supposed to do. But the words sounded powerful on the Captain's lips, and for this reason people generally remained impressed. He was now completely naked. Adamine considered his body, how everything about him was thin and long. His penis dangled almost halfway towards his knees. Captain Lucas caught her eyes on him. 'No, sister. Not on the Lord's day.'

'Yes,' Adamine whispered, chastened.

Just as no one truly understood Lucas's mystical words, no one would claim to truly understand the man. Stories surrounded him like a swarm of mosquitoes in June. People saw him everywhere. Rumour said that Lucas could split himself and be in five places at once. Most often people saw him after midnight, walking with a chain of padlocks around his neck, a machete in his hand. Adamine knew this story wasn't always untrue. She had seen the chain. Captain Lucas explained to her that it was for battling. It was part of his Duppy Conquering outfit.

'It is like the armour of God, Ada. When I wear it, angels make way for me and demons tremble. I tell you this, and I don't tell you to be a boasting man, but my greatest reputation is in a world different to the one most people can see. I talking bout the spirit world, Ada. Every spirit know bout me. Suppose I was to tell you stories, Ada? One time an old woman come to see me right here in this yard. Right here. She say to me she don't come for deliverance, she only come to testify. The sister tell me that she had been set upon by a real troublesome spirit. Then one day when she couldn't even rise up out of her bed, she did just get fed up to the brim. She shout to her daughter, "Daphne! Daphne! Call Captain Lucas to the house now!" Same time the demon jump out of her. Yes, Ada, you can say it again. Hallelujah. The sister tell me she could see the shape of the demon – a green lizard-like man. It turn to her and start beg, Don't call Captain Lucas! She see now that he was scared of me in truth, so she say to the lizard demon, Yes, I going to call him. I going to make him tell you, seven and seven and seven. For you is like a mighty delusion and a pestilence unto me. When the demon hear that, it fly from the house, and the sister swear she don't hear kemps from it again.'

As Lucas Gilles spoke, his words seemed to have, lingering on them, the trace of another accent. One rumour said he had come to Jamaica on a boat from Haiti. This was supposed to account for both the strength of his magic and the impenetrable silence he could sometimes slip into – as if he were a man who sometimes thought his thoughts in another language and could not be bothered to translate them. Adamine never asked him where he was from.

He pulled on an old pair of trousers to cover his nakedness, and he and Ada went out to the shed and began putting it back in order. The banner that read SEVEN HEAVENS, SEVEN OCEANS, SEVEN FIRES had fallen down in the middle of a particularly vigorous round of dancing; a basin of water had spilled; and the dirt that people carried in on their shoes was everywhere. The two worked in silence.

And then the silence was broken.

'Help!'

They stopped. The zinc fence around the balmyard was so high they couldn't see over it. They looked at each other. The voice was on the other side of the gate.

'Hello, please! Anybody inside there?' It was a woman. Her voice was the kind that had been broken somewhere in its centre. A banging started on the gate.

'Hello! Hello, please?'

'Ada, go and see what is the matter,' Lucas instructed.

Adamine went and opened the gate. A woman in her mid-twenties stood outside, but the resemblance between herself and Adamine stopped only at age. This woman was light-skinned, her hair pressed, and her clothes, while not lavish, still announced that she did not belong to the ghetto. She must have been desperate to get to the balmyard, Adamine thought, and she knew it had everything to do with the boy the woman was holding in her arms. He didn't seem to be conscious.

'You is the Mother of the yard? Oh God. Help him, please!' the woman blurted out. 'I had to take him out of the hospital. They wasn't doing nothing for him there. And him breathing get so shallow now, like ... like him soon going to ...'

'Come, come. Bring him in. We will see what we can do.'

Adamine knew that when she turned around, Captain Lucas would have transformed himself already. He was in his robes again, his head wrapped with strips of white and green and red cloth. His rod was in his hand. He stood by a bench in the middle of the yard.

'Go. Take the child over to Captain. He will know what to do.'

The woman walked across the yard slowly, Adamine nudging her forward from behind. Finally she rested the boy on the bench.

'Come, stand back now. Captain have to read up the boy. We can't stand too close.'

'He is my little brother,' the young woman volunteered. 'He fall sick two weeks now. Doctor don't even know ...'

Adamine hushed her. 'Don't say nothing just now. Let Captain do his work in peace.'

Captain Lucas was walking in slow circles around the boy, snapping his fingers as he went. His eyes were half closed. You could see the whites of them. 'Seven and seven and seven,' he muttered. Suddenly he opened his hands and ran his thin, long fingers up and down the air around the boy's body. His paused several times at a spot above the boy's heart, as if he had hit an invisible stone there.

'Mmmm. This lickle boy not sick in his body. Is bad spirit take him over, and he going to dead by midnight.'

The fair-skinned woman collapsed into Adamine's arms. She revived soon enough, a question immediately on her lips. 'What can be done for him? They tell me whatever can do for him would be here.'

Lucas shook his head solemnly. 'A very bad spirit indeed, my dear. Treatment would be expensive.'

'I can pay. I will pay you.' She took out folds of money from

130

her pockets, ten fifty-cent notes, and a few dollars. She began to open her purse. 'Whatever it takes.'

'But even more than money, miss, you need to start talking truth. You spake a lie on the seal just now, and lies give strength to evil spirits. It make the healing process very hard. Impossible sometime.'

'I don't think I understand you, sir.'

'You understand me very well, miss. Better you did just keep silent. But you tell a lie, and lying lips is an abomination here. Tell me who this boy is to you.'

The woman started to tremble, and then to cry.

'He is my son, sir. But he don't even know it. Nobody really know. I get pregnant when I was too young and my mother take him like he was her own child. He only know she as his mother.'

'Good, good. The truth. And the truth shall set you free. See now, the healing start already.' Lucas looked over at Adamine. 'My sister, lend me your scissors there a minute.'

Adamine handed him her scissors. Lucas began to snap them violently over the boy's heart and the boy's chest began to expand. It became so big, it was as if it would burst. Then the child began to cough.

'Now Ada, go get a clean white fowl. Do what needs to be done. Pour the blood into a bath. Make haste; it is a troublesome spirit we have here.'

Adamine ran to the fowl coop while Lucas recited from the Seventh Book of Moses. 'I, Lucas Gilles, a servant of God, call upon and conjure thee, Spirit Alymon, by the most dreadful words, Sather, Ehomo, Jehovah, Elohim, Volnah, Denach, Ophiel, Zophiel, Habriel, Eloha, Alesimus, Dileth, and by all the holiest words through which thou canst be conquered, that thou appear before me in a mild, beautiful human form, and fulfill what I command thee. Restore this boy, who has not lived the proper allotment of his days. Restore him back to health.'

Across from them, Adamine held down a white hen in a big

131

metal tub, squeezing its neck so tight it could not squawk. With her free hand, she cut off its neck. Free of its head, the body fluttered magnificently. Blood gushed into the tub. Adamine held the body until it was still. Then she took every basin of holy water from around the yard and poured them. Red water rose.

'Lord, I can't watch,' the young woman stammered as Lucas lifted the boy up from the bench and brought him over to the tub of blood.

'You don't have to watch,' Adamine said coolly. 'You done all you can for now. The boy need to stay in the bath overnight. Leave him here and come back in the morning.'

'No, no. I will wait. I can't just ...'

It was Lucas who snapped then. 'The Mother say you are to leave, ma'am! She know what she is talking. Now go.'

Adamine crossed the yard briskly and opened the gate wide. The young lady stumbled out. 'In the morning then?' she said sheepishly.

'In the morning,' Ada repeated, and for the second time that day she shut the gate with a bang.

✿

It was almost midnight. The boy was now asleep in Lucas's bed. He had groggily asked about his mama, and his sister Doreen, but then had dozed off again. Lucas and Ada were sitting outside, looking at a moon so low it seemed to rest on top of the red flag.

'It was a bad spirit that did take set on that lickle boy, but you do a good work today, Mother Ada.'

Adamine looked at him curiously. He was not a man known to give compliments, so she didn't know how to respond and simply nodded.

'A long time now I been thinking, Ada, you will make a good helpmeet unto a certain man. But you need a man who mighty in the Lord.'

Adamine felt her chest grow warm all of a sudden. She smiled. 'You talking in riddles, Captain,' but she understood his meaning. He was officially going to take her as his wife. She would move out of Bishopess Herbert's room and into the balmyard.

'You see how the moon shining bright tonight, Ada?'

'Yes, Captain. Like we can just jump right into it from here.'

Lucas reached over and let his long fingers rest on hers. 'When the moon sit that low, it mean you must break an egg and read up your future.'

'Break egg in holy water, you mean?' Ada looked at him sternly, as if the magic between them had been broken. 'No. I don't want to see no future for myself. I see enough future for everybody, and I don't like it. The future always come like a burden. Nothing good is there.'

Lucas allowed himself a rare smile. 'Not all the time, Ada. You must remember the people that you give warnings to is people who walking far from God. But for those of we who is like gentle sheep, who never go astray from the master, who live safe and sound under the rock, then we have nothing to fret bout.'

'Maybe so. But if that is true, then why read the future? Tomorrow come whether we want it to or not. I can tell you now what you have coming to you. A big brown coffin. Yes, you going to dead. And one day a coffin coming for me too. It don't need no messenger spirit from Heaven to tell us that. Leave the future where it is. It will come to us in its own time.'

'Ada,' Lucas's voice was firm, 'get the egg.'

She sulked. Sometimes she realised she felt too comfortable around him, spoke in too familiar a tone. She crawled into the fowl coop and the flock began their terrible squawking. She returned with an egg, white feathers all over her body. 'What now?' she snapped.

'Come, don't ruffle up your feathers with me.'

Despite herself, Adamine laughed.

'OK,' Lucas instructed. 'Crack the egg soft gainst a rock. Then you open it into the water.'

She cracked the egg and opened it over the basin of water. The yolk seemed to be its own full moon, and the white, which had been invisible, slowly gathered its colour, from the edges inward.

'What now?' Ada persisted.

'This part will take time. Best we sit down and wait.'

They sat, their knees touching.

'Ada. Now let us reason together. There is a brother in the Lord who name is Milton Dehaney ...'

'I never hear the name before.'

'Well, he was part of this band before he go to England. I get to understand that his life is now very hard over there. His wife, God bless her soul, was never very hearty from morning, a delicate thing she was. Now she has crossed the great Jordan river.'

'Oh bless her in her sleep,' Ada whispered.

'Indeed. But the brother write me now because he need a helpmeet. The work too much for one man ...'

'Yes, Captain.'

'Sometimes Ada, life take we somewhere we never expect. We must count that as blessing. As opportunity.'

'Yes, Captain,' Ada said again, but now it was her voice that was breaking at its centre. She saw that she really hadn't understood the Captain earlier. And sometimes the future came crashing into the present so fast, you lost your breath. It would have been good to have had a hint before, a warning. But a warning of what? What was Captain Lucas even saying?

As if reading her thoughts, he continued, 'All I am saying, Ada, is that whoever go to do this work in that far, far field will be doing a mighty work indeed. Milton will send money to pay for the fare ...'

'Oh,' Ada said softly. And then again, 'Oh,' understanding more. And a third time, 'Oh!'

She was angry. 'I see the whole plot now,' she hissed. 'He going to send money for a woman. And he going to send money for the band as well. He going to send money to you!'

'Things hard. The work have to get done somehow.'

'So you just plan to send me off like that? Like I is a prize whore? And you will take money for what you never did own? That is what we come to? A set of whores and thieves.'

The Captain spoke through gritted teeth.

'Ada, do not pass your place with me tonight. I will beat the devil out of you, so help me God. Now listen,' he grabbed her arm and held it painfully, 'me and Bishopess talk long about this ...'

'Bishopess Herbert know too?'

'Yes, and she agree. This is opportunity for everybody. Plenty of the sisters from the church would take this as fortune, so you best believe I not forcing this on nobody. So get up now, my daughter of Zion. Get up and look into the water. Tell me what shape your future has taken.'

He let go and reluctantly Adamine walked over to the basin.

She could have diagnosed her own condition in that moment. She had worked in the balmyard long enough, had become familiar with many ailments and could recite a whole taxonomy of illnesses. She could even tell you a disease by its Revivalist name, as well as the names the doctor in the hospital might use. There was, for instance, the condition she knew of as Deep-Sick, which in truth could be any number of things, but doctors called it 'chronic illness'; there was False-Belly, when a woman would look pregnant when she was not, and this was known to doctors as fibroids; there was Big-Foot, known otherwise as elephantiasis. But what Adamine experienced as she looked into the water was a simple case of Never-Expect, a condition known more generally as shock. The symptoms were the usual. She gasped, she felt a softness in her knees and she began to tremble. A future she had never dreamt of was suddenly laid out before her. She could see the sign clearly, even in the moonlight. The egg had formed itself into a boat. There was a stern, and a mast rising from the middle, and sails flapping in the wind. She imagined she could even see sailors on the deck. The moon above shone bright and the egg boat floated in the water as if it were an old ship sailing in the middle of the Antilles.

Lucas came up behind her. He held her gently by the waist and rested his chin on top of her head. He looked into the basin. 'Well, well. What I tell you, Ada? A journey is in your future to be sure.'

an instalment of a testimony spoken to the wind

Shhhhhhhh

I WANT TO tell you that is how it did go. I want to tell you I did leave Jamaica because I take the egg of a white fowl and break it into water and I see when it take the shape of a boat, just as how Father Noah did catch the vision of the ark. I want to say that is how the future did manifest itself unto me, and that it was bigger people than me who make the decision. I would love to say that in everything I was as innocent as the lamb, that I was sold into England like how Joseph was sold into Egypt. But it never happen like that. I never break no egg. Nobody did make up my mind for me. The vision I catch wasn't in no basin of water; it was in my own head all along, my own make-up fantasy. I leave Jamaica because my mind tell me to leave. Because everybody else was leaving and I decide to follow fashion. But God still could have did give me a warning. He could have did put a sign in my way. He could have did whisper in my ear, *stand firm, Ada, don't go.* What a crosses. The Warner Woman give warning to everybody, but who is there to give warning to the Warner Woman? Now draw yourself a long bench and I will tell you how the whole thing did really go. Three friends I have had in my life, and to tell you why I leave Jamaica, I must tell you their stories.

Shhhhhhhhh

My first friend was a woman named Sharon. She join the band because she was tired of dancing for the sons of men, and she begin to wonder what it would be like to

138

dance for God. And more than that, she wanted a place far away from the no-good dog she did shack up with. This man see her dancing onstage one night and he know that he sight his ticket, for he was a lazy sort of man. Him put sweet talk to her like men will do, him appear unto her like an archangel, and like a fool she believe him. Hell start when they get together for true. The man force Sharon to dance go-go more nights than she did want to, and then he call her slut and whore for doing it. He beat her too. A horrible kind of beating, because he would beat her careful. He don't want to mess up her skin. He need her skin to stay pure so she can earn more money for him dancing. He ongly beat her to make her cry. When she realise that was all he want, to see eye-water anointing her face, she begin to cry fast-fast so he don't end up throwing him fist into her belly or worse. Every night she pretend to cry, but after a time she realise she not pretending no more, like the alligator tears did open a door to her sadness. For life have more sorrows in it than people have water in their eyes, and if you could match your grief in tears, you surely would drown. So that is how Sharon end up at the Revival church. She find out what it mean to dance for the Lord, and she see that it was more sweet than dancing for the sons of men. At first, I never talk to her. Her eyes was always shut tight, and it would ongly take the first drum to knock for Sharon to lose herself trumping. When somebody get into spirit, nobody won't bother that person, for them is off into a whole nother world, and for many that is the ongly sweetness they get in life.

Shhhhhhhh

139

But one day I get a work to wash clothes at a house belonging to a Mr Leroy. It was one of those houses that look like it make out of concrete and light. I never know houses could build so strong and still have so much brightness inside. I get the work because it was near to Christmas time, and Mr Leroy did have plenty people visiting from foreign, so there was more clothes to wash than usual and more cooking and more cleaning, and the regular staff couldn't keep up. They put me outside by a washbasin and hand me a mountain of clothes, and a box of detergent, and a blue-bummer soap, and a bottle of bleach. But my eyes was fixed on the big house. I try to imagine myself living there, my foot up on a hassock and other people outside washing my dirty drawers. My mind start to drift and I begin to do foolishnesss. I put all the clothes in one tub – coloured and whites, and then I throw in detergent. Then I open the bleach bottle. Just like so I feel something slap me at the back of my neck. *Tough bitch! You have no sense? You don't see you bout to ruin the clothes? God help you if you mash up Mrs clothes that you can't afford!* I look round and see Sharon. Her face did set like she was regarding a mawga dog. I realise then that she was Mr Leroy's housekeeper and this is where she work during the day. She was looking at me so vex I know she don't recognise me. I don't have on my headtie. I don't have on no robes. I start to laugh. *In the balmyard you always walk pass me quiet and call me 'Mother'. You always have your eyes on the floor. But now you suddenly have strength to call me 'tough bitch'!* Sharon rub her eyes and look on me. She look on me again. Then she start to stammer. Lord have mercy! Prophetess! *Forgive me please, I never mean ...* I stop her. *You did well and mean what you say. And furthermore you was right. My mind did leave me and I was doing stupidness.*

140

That is where our friendship start. On Sundays we walk to the balmyard together and when service done we walk home hand in hand. Her fool-fool man was scared of me. I get used to things like that. A man may have muscle and fist, but if him don't have Jesus, if him only have evil in him heart, then he sure to avoid people like me, Warner Women, who could call down God on him raas. One day Sharon did come to me laughing. *Mother Ada, my man fraid of you like puss! Yesterday he ask me for money and I tell him I don't got a red cent. I see him getting vex and ready to put him hand on me again, but I just look up on the clock and act like I talking to myself. I say, I wonder what time Mother Ada coming back here? Mother, I barely done the sentence and him was halfway down the road. I don't even see when he did open the door to leave!* Me and Sharon was like sisters. One day I say to her, *tell me bout those clubs that you dance in. What is they like? They is really dens of evil?* Sharon think bout it a little and then say, *Not more than so. Every place in this world is a den of evil, but it don't got nothing to do with the place. It have everything to do with man.* I tell her something that I was thinking for a long time: *Sharon, I want to go with you one night.* She laugh. *No, no, Mother! Somebody like you can't go to a place like that.* I get vex. *But is you just tell me that nothing wrong with the place. Not more than so! Your words, not mine.* Sharon frown. *Come now, Mother. Don't act like you don't know what is what. If people see you there . . .* I pipe up quick, *If people see me there, I see them too.* But she wasn't convinced. *Is not the same. Other people can do what you can't do. And if word ever get back to Captain, he beat you to a pulp — beat you worse than my man beat me.* I tell her, *I can handle Captain.* And I serious too. *I want to come one night. I not a woman to waste my words. I ongly say what I mean.* She frown deeper

141

this time because she know I was serious and that I was stubborn to a fault. *All right. All right. Next Monday night I will take you, but only if I get you ready. Kill me dead,* she say, looking up, making her oath to the sky, *I not going to make nobody realise that is really you.*

Shhhhhhhhh

On Monday night I was sitting in Sharon room and she put on every kind of powder and every kind of paint on my face. I don't even recognise my own self. I feel like some alien from outer space. Then she give me a green outfit to put on. The thing was so tight that if I had a fifty cent in my pocket, you would see Marcus Garvey face clear clear, and him would be fighting for air. Now that I in all this get-up, I can't believe I put myself up to it. I start worry but Sharon is the one who confident now. *Not a soul will recognise you, Mother. Look on yourself . . . you look like a woman!* I ask her, *So what I did look like before?* She never even pause. *Before you did look like somebody that man was fraid of. Tonight you look like somebody a man would touch.* So we head out. She take me to the club, and Jesus-Saviour-pilot-me! I see things that night that appear to me like a miracle. I know it wasn't God in that place, not the same God who we did know in the balmyard, but what I see on that night was just as wonderful as when the Saviour turn water to wine, or when he make the blind man see. When Sharon start to dance, the Spirit of the Psalmist was in her. Lickle by lickle all her clothes drop off and she stand up on that stage naked as the day her mama did birth her. Sharon spread her legs wide and show the whole place her woman-parts. All the man them start to whistle. Then, suppose I tell you what happen next. Even

142

now I don't too believe it. Sharon roll a ganja spliff, cool cool, and she light it. And where else that girl put it but right up into her coochie. Eh eh! I never know woman-parts could be so strong. Sharon could do things with hers that make me feel like me was not a proper woman myself. She smoke the spliff with her coochie – inhale it deep, then the lips of her woman-parts open up and clouds of smoke just come out. The men start behaving bad that time. They clap and give her one whole heap of money – like all of the day's earning did gone to Sharon in that moment. Later on when we was walking home I couldn't stop myself from laughing. I hold Sharon hand like she was my woman, and she hold my hand like she was my man, and I start to feel happy in a way that maybe I was not happy before. I never before have a sister. I did say a prayer that night that things would stay like that for ever.

Shhhhhhhhh

Then one day Sharon say to me, *Mother, nothing in this country for me no more. I going to leave when I can.* The news break my heart, but it didn't shock me. People did leave whenever they get the chance. So I just ask her simple when she thinking of leaving, and where she planning to go. Sharon get silent. The silence stretch so long that I wonder if she hear me. I ask again, and get back silence a second time. A bad feeling start come over me. I ask her a third time and maybe vexation was in my voice. *When you leaving, Sharon? How long now you been planning this?* She answer at last, *Mother, I sorry I never tell you before. Is tomorrow I leaving.* And that was the last I ever see her. And those was the last words I ever catch from her lips. I was vex and sad and

143

angry and so many different things at one time. I can't even tell you when I did start running. That is what heartache do. It possess your body like a spirit and make it do foolishness, make you run away from your friends and don't tell them goodbye. The worse thing is Sharon never did reach foreign. That night the man must have seen her packing and know it was all over. So he beat her. He give her the beating that he never able to give her before. He don't stop when he hear her crying. He don't care that this time him is bruising her, making her skin turn purple and red. When he finish, he himself walk to the police station, cool as ice, with his hands in the air, and tell the corporal, *you all best lock me up now, cause I just done kill the bitch.* When they find Sharon they only know it was she because him tell them it was she. Plenty days my mind run on Sharon even now. I think if grief never take over my body, I would have been able to tell her goodbye. We would have hugged each other like sisters and cry unto each other's shoulders. For who knoweth the hour that is appointed unto man and woman?

Shhhhhhhhh

The next friend I did have was Doreen. I meet her by buck-ups, if you call such things buck-ups – I would call it an arrangement made by God. It was He who had been whispering hard in my ears that day. The message come to me like the most complicated one I ever get. God telling me he want me to go to a place, but I never hear of this place before. Still, I decide to be obedient. I wrap my head and tie a scissors round my waist. Then I start walking and ask the spirits to show me the way. I get lost three times. The way confusing and whichever spirit

144

whispering in my ear don't know left from right. I was almost ready to call it quits, for the Lord couldn't say I never tried, but at last I come to the house. People did form a big crowd outside, all of them silent like they was waiting on something. When they catch sight of me coming, it was like this is what they was waiting for. The women find permission to bawl and they start to shout out in the streets, *Lawd, he dead now! See the Warner Woman coming! Him dead now for sure!* I don't pay them no mind. I walk into the house and into the room where a woman was wiping cold sweat from the brow of her little boy. His eyes was closed. His skin look grey to me. Him look like he fast asleep, but he trembling something terrible in that sleep. I see that this lickle boy is no more than six years old and my heart break for him. The woman who I take to be his mama look up to me now, she hold on to the bed like she trying to stop herself from faint. She try to say something but no words coming out. She get up and this time she faint for true, right into my arms. I had to fan her until she come back to herself. She mumbling. *I think I was ready for this, but I not ready. Lord take the case!* I talk to her soft, *Calm down, Mama, calm down. God not ready neither.* Her neck spin right round and she look up on me funny. *Four doctors I been to already. Four. And all of them tell me the same thing. They tell me nothing can do for him. They tell me him is way past the point of help.* I tell her, *Doctor don't know a goddamned thing. Nothing wrong with the boy in his body. Is bad spirit was put on him.* I stand up now and take the scissors in my hands and I start to cut the air above the boy's head. I cut and clear and cut and clear. I get vicious with the air like I was cutting cane for buckra. The boy start to cough. This is the first sound I hear from him and I know him coming back to life. I start speak in

145

language. I call Satan by all the awful names I know him by, and I chase him out of the room. I call Rutibel by all the names I know him by, and chase him out too. The mother can't believe it. Her boy getting better right in front her eyes. *Go*, I tell her. *Get a fowl quick as you can. The healing don't complete yet. We have to give the lickle boy a bath.* She run out and come back, a green and red fowl squawking in her hands. I take it out to the yard and put it in a bucket. I read the 65th Psalm. *O God of our Salvation, who art the confidence of all the ends of the earth, and of them that are afar off upon the sea.* I read the 118th Psalm. *Let Zion now say — his mercy endureth for ever. It is better to trust in God than trust in man. The Lord is my strength and my song. This is the Lord's doing and it is marvellous in our eyes.* I cut the fowl neck, quick so it can't make a sound. The blood start to pour. I dip my finger and go inside to make the sign of the cross on the boy's head. We pour the rest of the blood in a bath and put him inside it. Then I call on Miriam and Raphael, on Michael and Gabriel. I hear a fluttering of wings like the spirit of God and I know everything is going to be all right.

Shhhhhhhhh

Bishopess used to say, when fowl drink water him say thank God, but when man drink water him don't say nothing. But the lickle boy's mama did know to give proper thanks. Her name was Doreen, and she did grow in a higher society than I was used to. She did go to a Methodist church, and although she know bout Revival, she don't ever jump it. Still, she make her way to the Band of the Seventh Fire, and she pay for a thanksgiving table so big it did make all goat for miles tremble. Three

146

days straight we was giving praises, and neither the curry goat nor the rum did run out once in that time. The trumping and the drumming take us to regions of Heaven we never venture in before. Doreen dance with the band for the three days, and she lift her hands unto God Almighty, and tears was pouring down her face, and she say thank you for sending your servant, and giving life abundant back unto my son.

Shhhhhhhhh

I think that was the last I would ever see her. After all, she live in a whole nother community, far up on a higher branch, she custom to eating a sweeter fruit. But one day I reach home and there she was, outside the gate, waiting with the patience of Job, she and her lickle boy, Jevon. She stand up when she see me coming and she say, *Miss, I think you are like our Guardian Angel, and God knows in these days we need all the angels we can get. I don't want us to lose touch.* Some nights if Doreen had somewhere to go, she take Jevon over and make him sleep in the same room with me and Bishopess Herbert. I would sit him down and learn him many things. Sometime he ask me, *why they call your church Revival?* And I would tell him what he was never tired of hearing, *it is because we is a people who can shake off grave dirt. We is a people who can come back from the dead. And you is one of us too because you yourself did come back from a deep and awful sleep. I found you dead, Jevon. But guess what? You revive.* Me and Doreen become combolo, the bestest of friends. She get to know me as Ada, and not as no Warner Woman. I talk to her like an ordinary woman will talk to her ordinary woman friend. Plenty evenings we just sit there together, simple with each other, and years pass by like that. The evening

147

come when she say to me, *Ada, nothing in this country for we.*
I leaving. I taking Jevon and we leaving. I was ready for that one.
I nod and say to her, *come then, my sister, I will light a candle*
and pray for you. And I make sure the eye-water don't spill
from my eyes, and that my voice hold steady and strong.
I pray that Father God in Heaven would hold my friend
Doreen by the hand, and that He would continue to grow
up Jevon who He did love enough to revive. I pray that
they would journey well.

Shhhhhhhhh

My last friend was Lucas Gilles. Everybody in the band
call him Captain, but I call him Lucas. Just like after a
time everybody in the band call me Mother, but he call
me Ada. We understand that we was ongly special people
when we in the band, when we wearing our robes, and
when we have our head in wraps. Without that we was
the same people who Babylon trample down like grass.
Lucas, mighty Captain, he work his days as a simple yard
boy. He say the mister of the house was not so bad. The
mister talk to him kindly and come Christmas time him
was even known to share a quart of rum with Lucas.
There was even one time when the mister and his friends
ongly make three, and dominoes need four, so he call
Lucas unto the veranda and ask him to play a hand with
them. Lucas say he feel like he was somebody that night,
more than just the fellow who cut the hedges and wash
the cars and nail up what needed nailing up. But Lucas
say the Mrs was as bad as the Mister was good. She call
out to Lucas like how you might call after a mawga dog.
When the Mrs see the helper serve Lucas him lunch on a
plate, she bawl down the helper and say she can't be

wasting her good good china like that. From then on Lucas get his lunch in an old ice cream dish. The Mrs try to crush him dignity and I wonder how any woman could look on a man like Lucas, with his blue-black skin, and not see that he was somebody mighty, that he was somebody deserving of respect. I wonder that she couldn't see what a powerful man he was, or maybe she see it, and that is why she try to rub it out. Some nights Lucas come to my bed and he just want to be inside me, both of us just man and woman together. And when our bodies rub up gainst each other, I learn to be quiet even when it feel sweet. One time he touch me and say, *you can make noise. I sorry I hit you that time. It was wrong of me.* Sometimes when we done our man and woman business, he hold me to him chest and start to talk. You would never expect the Captain to talk those things that he did talk, but he wasn't talking as Captain. He was talking as Lucas. He say to me, *Ada, we is an abandoned people. Some days I feel we is abandoned by God.* And some nights I did tell him what I was feeling too. Like one night when my fingers was wrinkled up from washing so much clothes the whole livelong day, I tell him, *Lucas, this island don't have nothing for me. Sometimes I want to leave.* And him say to me, *I know you would say this one day.* He hold me close to his chest then and I feel sad cause his chest don't feel so strong as it normally do. He say to me, *I think I know a man that can help you get over there and settle.* That time my chest fall like him own did fall before, and at the same time it did swell up with the future. And I telling you this long testimony so that you know how I come to England. Not because God did send me. Not because Lucas did send me. It was something in my own heart. It was something I did want to do.

149

I did forget the song we did always sing — *Any-anywhere that the army go, Satan follow.*

Shhhhhhhhh

What I come to find out is this: God never love me. For it is written, which man would give unto his son a stone if the son did ask for bread? And which man would give unto his son a snake if the son did ask for fish? And so if we who are so evilous and wicked know how to give good things, then how much more will Father God give unto us? But I ask God for something better than Spanish Town, Jamaica, and he give me this country where I have tilled a hard ground.

The Middle of the Story

Every book must begin somewhere, but it begins in different places for different people. If you are the reader, then things get going at Chapter One, the first sentence – *Once upon a time there was a leper colony in Jamaica.* But for the writer, the book would have begun somewhere else altogether.

Maybe you have already seen the beginnings of a book; maybe you have been in a café and you were just about to pay for your coffee and your croissant when a man muscled his way to the counter and asked for a napkin and a pen, please, please, quick! He would have grabbed the items and run back to his seat. And you would have understood: a thought had just perched itself on the tip of this man's imagination, singing its teasing song, *Catch me if you can.* The man would have known the song and the bird; he would have met them before, and would have lost them before, as we are all known to lose feathery bits of inspiration. For this reason, people are known to walk around with a variety of traps – cameras, video-recorders, sound-recorders, notepads, sketchpads, scissors.

The reader begins the journey at Chapter One, but the writer will have begun somewhere else, on something like a napkin, where the bird was first caught. Every book starts like this, from something small. But when it has all been written down, when the story has stretched to its full size, then the writer will step back, and he will find to his surprise that the small bird has been swallowed and is now in the belly of a larger beast. That is to say, the beginning of the story is now somewhere in the middle. And this is where you have finally arrived, at that place in the middle of the story, which is really to say, you have finally come to the beginning.

At last you have found your way to the three pink slips of paper from which the present story has sprung. These three papers are official. The British government has dubbed them: a Form 12; a subjoined Statement of Particulars to the Form 12; and finally, a Form 2.

When I received these three forms they smelled of dust and, I imagined, of the metal drawer in which they had been filed for so long. They were old and thin and ready to disintegrate, as if I could have held them up to a bright light and watched them become dust, watched them float away through my fingers. I wondered whether that would be a good thing, whether the story suddenly became part of the air, something we could breathe in and breathe out. I had to handle these documents carefully. A week went by and I didn't want to risk even looking at them. I took them everywhere, mind you – they were that precious. But at last I managed to get them laminated.

Safe now between barriers of plastic, I finally laid the pages out and looked at them properly. This book could finally begin. These three forms were heavily stamped; boxes and circles of green and red ink, and signatures everywhere. In a certain light they might have even appeared festive; by any other light they looked as official and unfriendly as the job they were meant to do. These forms were produced in order to secure the taking away and locking up of people – the sectioning of men who had fallen into the habit of pulling out their members in public parks or on buses, happily masturbating, oblivious to their audience; of women who babbled to themselves and kept on asking for Harold, or Jimmy, or Michael, long-dead husbands, as if they were just sitting in the room next door; of the girl whose eyes had suddenly begun to dance in terror around her sockets, and who had woken up believing the world was in danger from an invasion of giant, blue ants; of the boy who had to be kept far away from his mother's migraine tablets, and also from knives, because he shook her awake one night to show her a crudely slashed wrist and giggled as he told her, 'Dying is sweet, Mam, I wish I could die every day.'

It took some time to secure these specific forms, being government records. I had to get help from a friend who wrote a letter that sounded very threatening, and who then signed it as my attorney. At first I hadn't even been thinking of a book, but when I finally received them, and had them laminated, and arranged them before me, something like the evidence from a trial – let's call them Exhibits 1, 2 and 3 – I could see that a story was emerging.

EXHIBIT 1

Parish of Saint Osmund
in the County of Warwickshire.
Mental Health Act, 1959, Ch. 5, Sec. 16, Schedule 2,
Form 12. Order of Reception for a Lunatic.

I, <u>Sgt V.C. Mitchells</u>, having called to my assistance, <u>Dr David O Strachan</u>, of <u>107 Clarence Drive, SE</u>, a duly qualified medical practitioner, and being satisfied that <u>Pearline Portious</u> of <u>Ramside and of no known occupation</u> is an indigent in ~~receipt of relief [or in~~ such circumstances as to require relief for h<u>er</u> proper care and maintenance] and that the said <u>Pearline Portious</u> is a ~~lunatic [or an idiot, or a~~ person of unsound mind] and a proper person to be taken charge of and detained under care and treatment, hereby direct you to receive the said <u>Pearline Portious</u> as a patient into your asylum.

153

This first form is duly signed by Sergeant V.C. Mitchells. His signature is a looping flourish, not exactly what I would have expected of a police officer annoyed with paperwork, who just wants to be done with it. The form is dated the 14th day of November 1972, and is addressed to the Superintendent of the Mental Hospital for the County of Warwickshire at Saint Osmund. I put it aside and move on to the next form.

EXHIBIT 2

Statement of Particulars
STATEMENT of Particulars referred to
in the above or annexed orders
The following is a statement of particulars relating
to the said <u>Pearline Portious-Dehaney</u>

- Name of patient, with Christian name at length . .
  . . . . Pearline Portious-Dehaney
- Sex and age . . . . 32, female
- Married, single or widowed . . . . married
- Rank, profession, or previous occupation (if any) .
  . . . . no occupation
- Religious persuasion . . . . none
- Residence at or immediately previous to date hereof
  . . . . unknown
- Whether first attack . . . . yes
- Age on first attack 32
- When and where previously under care and treatment
  as a lunatic, idiot, or person of unsound mind . .
  . . . . unknown

154

- Duration of existing attack . . . . 4 hours
- Supposed cause . . . . of West Indian origin
- Whether subject to epilepsy . . . . probable
- Whether suicidal . . . . undetermined
- Whether dangerous to others, and in what way . . .
  . . . . threatening and aggressive
- Whether any near relative has been afflicted with insanity . . . . unknown
- County to which lunatic is chargeable . . . .
  . . . . . Warwickshire

I know immediately that I will come back to this form again and again, reading it for what it says and also what it doesn't say. Already two things strike me as peculiar. Religious persuasion ... none. This makes me think of Christopher Columbus, who by complete accident having sailed his way into the Caribbean, wrote back to his king and queen to say no form of religion was to be found in the Caribbean or among its people. I have always thought that a strange blindness, not to see what was so magnificently apparent. But I have been to Jamaica and heard a story: a Jamaican young man who had lived in England for years went back to visit. He saw some crabs walking about and in an affected way asked his father, "Oh Father, what are those?" But when the crab bit his finger he hollered, "Pupa, de crab a bite me!" In the same way, when Columbus experienced a Caribbean storm he would call out to God by the name he was commonly called in those islands, Hurican!

The second thing that intrigues me about this form is the casual manner in which the mental health worker has written down a theory of 'supposed cause'. On most forms this space would have been left blank, or else it would have been a guess hazarded by a close family member – stress at work, spouse committed suicide,

155

and so on. I did not know that being of West Indian origin was sufficient cause for madness. And yet I have always known the statistics: the highest percentage of schizophrenic patients in British asylums was always West Indian migrants, as if only the very crazy had bothered to climb aboard ships and sail to the Mother Country.

I used to think that this had everything to do with Columbus's blindness, or something like it – that unable to recognise what was so deeply religious in the Caribbean people flooding her shores, Britain had misread them as being mad or deranged. Their tambourines and their hats and their habit of speaking in tongues seemed like lunacy to Britain.

There was a time when I was confident in this analysis. Some days I was even angry. I would think of words such as injustice, arrogance, institutionalised racism. But then one day, having the time, and the money, and the inclination, I went to Jamaica. There I met several people who on hearing my accent, would say, 'Oh! You is from England? Well, let me tell you something, I have a auntie who did go there and she and the whole lot of them that did go to the Mother Country, every raas one of them, mad as shad! You hear me, son? Mad as bloodclawt shad!'

EXHIBIT 3

Parish of Saint Osmund in the County of
Warwickshire.
Mental Health Act, 1959,
Ch. 5, Sec. 16, Schedule 2, Form 8.

CERTIFICATE OF MEDICAL PRACTITIONER
In the matter of Pearline Portious-Dehaney of
 Ramside in the county of Warwickshire of
no occupation, an alleged lunatic.

I <u> Dr David Strachan </u> the undersigned, do certify
as follows:

1. I am a person registered under the Medical Act and
   am a person in the actual practice of the medical
   profession.

2. On the <u>23rd</u> day of <u>November 1972</u>, at <u>Saint Osmund
   Mental Hospital</u>, in the county of <u>Warwickshire</u>, I
   personally examined <u>Pearline Portious-Dehaney</u> and
   came to the conclusion that she is a person of
   unsound mind and a proper person to be taken charge
   of and detained under care and treatment.

3. I formed this conclusion on the following grounds,
   viz –

   a) Facts indicating insanity observed by myself at
      the time of examination:
      <u>Patient is by turns both talkative and spirited,</u>
      <u>then sulky and withdrawn. In her spirited moments</u>
      <u>she claims awareness of an old man with a twisted</u>
      <u>leg floating somewhere near her ear. She calls</u>
      <u>this man Papa Legba and says that he gives her</u>
      <u>'warnings'. When asked about these 'warnings'</u>
      <u>they turn out to be rather alarming – apocalyptic</u>
      <u>notions of floods and earthquakes and the like.</u>
      <u>The patient also insists that her name is Adamine</u>
      <u>Bustamante. When confronted with the evidence of</u>
      <u>her passport and other papers found on her person,</u>
      <u>the patient makes strange sucking sounds with her</u>
      <u>teeth and withdraws again into her dour mood.</u>

   b) Facts communicated by others:
      <u>Patient was apprehended in front of the Council</u>
      <u>House at Victoria Square where she had been making</u>
      <u>a spectacle of herself. Several eyewitnesses</u>
      <u>described her as shaking violently as if in the</u>

middle of an epileptic fit, and shouting out a
series of the aforementioned warnings. Sgt Mitchells was sent out to her when she became so
loud that she disrupted and effectively ended a
sitting of the council.

From these three forms I began to reconstruct events; a whole narrative was unfolding before me. People emerged from the ink of their own hands, and I even thought how ethical this was, the way people were writing their own way into the story. Sergeant V.C. Mitchells' handwriting, for instance, is dark and heavy, as if he were a man who pressed down a little too hard on his pen. I could just imagine him, paused between each letter, the pen still resting on the paper, as he mouthed and practised the words he was about to write down. A man of deliberation. I conjured him then to be a middle-aged man with a round belly on which he could rest his hands. I could see him, from the distance of thirty years, sitting in a red armchair in Council House in Birmingham.

Large teak doors that seem as if they should belong to a church are closed. A meeting is underway and it is Sergeant Mitchells' duty to 'guard the perimeters'. It is easy work, more ceremony than function, and involves only sitting down for three hours, nodding with deference to the councillors as they walk in and out, self-important in their gowns and their heavy chains of office. There would have been a time when Mitchells would have resented this kind of work, but now, only two years away from retirement, he doesn't mind it. For three hours he is required only to play with his buttons, to rub his hand across his bald pate, to observe for the hundredth time the different plates on the wall. He is so intent on passing the time in this manner that when the commotion outside begins, a sound as loud as an air raid siren that shakes the whole of Council House and rattles two of the decorative plates off the wall. Mitchells' first instinct is to press himself deeper into his chair. He remembers then that it wasn't retirement that slowed him down. He has always been slow. He has never had that instinct common to all good police officers, a natural urge to run towards a scene, towards gunfire and screaming, while everyone else is running away.

The sound outside is escalating. Mitchells thinks, what the devil is wrong with that woman? He can tell that much – that it is a woman. And also that she is black. He can tell from the sound and shape of her words, the way she is pronouncing 'flood', something deep and resonant in the vowels; he imagines this is how a large copper bell would pronounce the word if it could. And also the way she says eart'quake, losing the 'h', and how this word in particular seems to practise its meaning, causing everything to shake. Mitchells begins to think what a different place Birmingham has become – first hit by bombs, and then by immigrants. I imagine he would have fancied himself a congenial, liberal kind of man. Perhaps one of his best mates, Ezekiel, was as coloured as they came, chocolate for skin, and he and Ezekiel would have shared many pints together. Mitchells was not one of those who thought the coloureds should have bloody well stayed where they came from. Fair is fair, he might tell you, they fought for the Mother Country when others just sat in their offices the whole bloody time. And after the war there was all that rubble to be picked up, and train-tracks to be relaid, and houses to be rebuilt. There were jobs aplenty. Mitchells would tell you there were more jobs than people. But even Mitchells would concede that although there were places for them to work, there were no places for them to live. So the new immigrants ended up living, sometimes, twenty to a house. Mitchells would have been a bit green in those days, and the influx of people, many of them with tempers as hot as fire, would have made his work difficult. He wouldn't have liked having to go to their houses, sorting out their squabbles, decoding their language and writing down statements which, for him, were largely guess-work.

'Hawficer, a dead de bwoy deserve fi dead.'

'Pardon me, ma'am?'

'Hawficer! Oh Jesus Christ have mercy pon a sinner like me! Look pon mi good good son, fallen!'

'Pardon me, ma'am?'

'Hawficer, mi never do a ting more dan stan up like dis wid de pickaxe in mi hand. Is him come run up into it.'

'Pardon me, sir?'

So Mitchells knows that this woman shouting Flood and Eart'quake and breaking plates with just her voice is one of these immigrants, and is glad to be inside, glad that he doesn't have to face her, glad that he doesn't have to try breaking through the storm of her words, saying 'Ma'am, ma'am, please can you calm down.'

But then the teak doors groan open. Sergeant Mitchells jumps to his feet. The Lord Mayor flounces towards him. 'What the blazing hell is going on out there?'

'S-sir, your w-w-worship ...' Mitchells begins and feels like a novice again rather than a sergeant just two years shy of retirement.

'W-w-w-well, do something!' the mayor shouts, mocking the sergeant's sudden stammer. 'That ruckus out there is an utter disgrace!'

So Mitchells would have had to do what he had never liked doing. He had to run towards a commotion instead of running away from it.

Outside, Victoria Square has come to a standstill, and Mitchells can see her now, the woman causing this great disturbance. She is wearing what can only be described as a crown – a red and white crown that rises from her head like a mountain. In a few minutes he will manage to pull this elaborate headpiece from her, and he will see then that it is only strips of cloth braided together. Everyone

160

in the square is frozen by the woman's performance. Her hands are spread wide and she is spinning, her head dipping and coming back up. He feels dizzy just watching her. But for all her turning and dipping, the woman's voice remains steady. Mitchells even wonders whether it really is her own voice because at times it seems not to come from her, but from above. It is as if Heaven is shouting with her, or that she is shouting with Heaven.

The sergeant thinks that in all his years he has never seen madness like this before – for this is a madness that is beautiful and terrible and powerful all at once. He begins to walk towards the woman and feels as if he is stepping into the centre of a hurricane. As big a man as he is, he feels he has to hold himself together so he won't blow away. He approaches slowly, squinting.

And then suddenly he believes he is going to drown. He believes the earth is going to swallow him. He believes blood is going to rain from the sky and the moon will turn into red. The closer he gets, the more he accepts everything she is shouting. He wants to turn back and warn everyone else too, that right here and right now, in the cold of Birmingham, there will be a natural disaster the like of which has never been seen. But Mitchells has worked in the force for too long and is only two years away from retirement, so he pushes the thoughts from his head. He knows these are her thoughts, and he doesn't stop to consider how they have been planted so firmly in his own mind. He is finally in front of her. She keeps on spinning. Her cries are still getting louder. He cannot hear himself when he begins to speak. 'Ma'am. Please, ma'am. Can you calm down for me? Calm down I say! MA'AM!'

✹

But, dear reader – if I may address you so directly – there is something that happens when the writer begins to reveal himself. When he suddenly declares himself as 'I'. It compels him, quite

161

frankly, towards honesty. So what if I were to tell you that I am not actually sure where this book begins. It may have been the three pink slips of paper I have just described. But then, it may have been before.

What if I confess that maybe, just maybe, the beginning of this story is the day of my own beginning. 18 March 1976.

I was born in Warwickshire, England.

I was born, perhaps as you were, in a hospital.

But I'm afraid that mine was no ordinary hospital. It was a mental asylum. I was born to a patient there – a woman registered under the name Pearline Portious-Dehaney. I have searched for this woman a long time. They tell me she was of unsound mind.

They tell me that during labour she had been tranquillised so heavily that she did not push or grunt or do anything at all. She just lay there.

They tell me it was the midwife who reached in and pulled me out of the womb, almost as if she were rescuing me.

When I was born, I was beautiful. My skin was the exact colour of a clear sky. I was beautiful, and blue, but I was, of course, dead.

And then something strange happened. My crazy, crazy mother, my mother who had seemed so useless, even to herself, suddenly raised her head and the glaze lifted from her eyes. She spoke up. But she was speaking a language that no one knew, such odd syllables which she brought together like an incantation. And whatever it was that she said, it caused a shiver to travel up everyone's arms, up their necks, and a sharp coldness slapped them in the centre of their brains, freezing them.

My mother's words froze everyone in the room except me. For me, her words were a melting. I opened up my lifeless mouth and gulped a first portion of air. The colour of the sky poured away from my skin.

They tell me I was born dead, but when my mother said this

thing, this strange unpronounceable thing, it was like a miracle, like a Revival; I suddenly became alive.

You see, every story stretches in two directions – creeping into a past, galloping towards a future. And every writer is searching for something – himself, his mother, the truth.

an instalment of a testimony spoken to the wind

Shhhhhhhh

EVERY DAY HAVE its order, and every hour its own arrangement. That is how to keep yourself in a right and proper
mind, by knowing what is what, and what things belong
to which time, otherwise your life is a giant darkness, a
great madness. It is like an Apocalypse. Listen, Apocalypse
is the day when you wake to find that straight after 6
o'clock comes 9 o'clock – no 7 or 8 in between. Apocalypse is the day when the sun rise from the west and set
in the east. Or Apocalypse is a day like today – like an
extra day of the week, a day that don't normally come
but when it does it is like bat wings and darkness rushing
towards you. You can't do a thing. You just stay there,
simple and fool, and your mind stop working. I feel like
I slipping. I feel like the ground underneath me is oil and
I can't stand up. I feel the madness rising in me again,
but I praying hard. I sending these words to you as
always, but I sending some up to Heaven as well. Lord,
deliver me. Lord, deliver me, because everything has lost
its order. Hear and believe what I saying to you – if you
don't mind sharp, on your own day of Apocalypse, you
will go stark raving mad. You who never think you could
end up walking the road naked, begging money from car
window, you frighten to know you will do that and
worse.

Shhhhhhhhh

Before today, the shape of my days was simple. Mr Writer
Man would wake me at around 6.30 in the morning and

166

set a cup of green tea before me and a cup of coffee before himself. We would be in the living room, the steam rising from the cups, and the tape-recorder between us. He would allow me to talk, sometimes for as long as an hour and then I don't know how he decide, but it come a time when he touch the tape-recorder and say, *all right, Ada, that's enough for today*. He pick up the recording machine and go into a room that have his computer and plenty books rising up to the ceiling. When he in there he don't pay me no mind. I think it is like another world to him. The phone might be ringing. The house couldly all be burning down. He wouldn't care. The door not shut but he still shut off to everything. He play the recording a little bit at a time, then he type things into the computer. Sometimes I pass and notice he not listening or typing; he ongly staring like a man might stare at an angel or a white dove, as if a message is out there and he praying for revelation. Now, whenever he gone into that room to do his work, I pick up a key and take myself out of the apartment. I go down the stairs and out into the streets. The roads have their names but I don't stop to read them. I can tell you though which road make the shape of an S, and which one is just a straight line with the first part wide and the last part narrow. And I can tell which one have red bricks in the middle, and which one is black gravel the whole way. I walk the same route always and sit in the same park and watch the same heron in the tree stretching forth his two wings like maybe he think he is the Saviour and him want to be crucified. On the walk back it is always the same people who line up at a bakery called Gregg. The place have a smell of cheese and sugar and although I don't eat cheese as a rule, and I never frighten for sugar, the smell still make my belly complain for hunger. When I reach back to the apartment Mr Writer Man will be sitting at the table eating bread and butter and eggs. He will nod for me to join him, so I sit down and we eat in silence. I begin to wonder if the ongly way we can ever talk is to have a machine between us, if we can ongly exchange words if a record of those words is kept. Most mornings he just stare at me and it make me feel funny. In turn I stare at the bread, or at the butter, or at everything but him. I act like I don't notice his eyes. They is green like the underside of a banana leaf. He just keep looking as if he hoping something will happen but nothing ever happen. Another time it is me who stare at him, because sometimes is like a ghost will pass over his face, like a shadow of something I did once know. I stare at him whenever I see this and he now is the one to pretend he don't notice me, but his whole body change in these moments. It get tight and relaxed and nervous all at once, and you would think he is offering his whole self to me, like a lamb who want to be found worthy. I just stare and is like his body finally give up and become downcast. At last him will get up and touch me on my shoulders and that is his way of saying goodbye. He leave to go wherever it is him go off to in the days. I don't ask him nothing before he leave, not even to know when he coming back.

Shhhhhhhh

When he leave I always do the same thing. I did feel like a burglar at first, but now I don't feel no way. It is just the shape of my day. I go into the same room with the same computer and all the books and I sit down in his chair. I take up the papers that him print out that morning and I read back everything that he write. When somebody write out your story, to read it is like a forgetting and also it is like a memory. At first I forget this story is supposed to be bout me. I read it just like I would read any Anansi story. I turn the pages to find out what going to happen next. But a little later I reading and I shaking with vexation. All on a sudden I know this woman him writing bout is me, and these people he telling untruths bout is people I did used to know. When time that happen I keep thinking – what right this boy think he have to change it all up? Who make him god of anything? But when I think that I get a strange thought. I stop to wonder if he might really be God after all. I have seen paintings of the Messiah. He is a man with long curly black hair and what they call olive skin, and his eyes is green like the underside of a banana leaf. And so I wonder if Mr Writer Man might be Jesus after all. And not simply because of the way him look, but also the way he sometimes write down parts of my life that I never did tell him. I start to consider the woman at the well who the Saviour did meet. Him tell her to her face, *thou hast had five husbands and the one you living with now is not one of them.* And same so, the woman get fraid and run off to tell the town, *Come, see a man who tell me all the things that I ever did, is this not the Christ?*

Shhhhhhhhh

What I trying to tell you is this – that every morning when I go into the room and I read out my story as it is written by Mr Writer Man, sometimes it vex up my spirit for true, but it soothe me at the same time. And it heal me. For is like the Saviour telling me all the things I ever

169

did, and giving me back my whole life. The parts that did fall away, they rise back again. Roads that did fade into dust was being restored. This man don't tell the story straight. He put in all kinds of lies. But every lie open the door to a truth. What I trying to tell you is this – that maybe I was ready to give thanks unto this man. I was ready to give thanks to him for giving me back all I think I did lose. But take heed, Children of Zion. Take heed. When things going too well, when you think God has remembered you at last, God will remember to forget you again.

Shhhhhhhhh

When the boy leave the apartment this morning, I get up as usual and go to the room. I surprise to find the door shut. I try to turn the handle but the door don't give no way. I never know before the door could shut let alone that it could lock so tight. I start to shake it but ongly my body was rocking. It come to me then that it was my own self on the other side of that door. Mr Writer Man decide to keep me away from myself. I now know for sure something I did come to suspect. Mr Writer Man know my habits. He know I was coming to read what him write bout me. But today he write something that he don't care for me to read. I start to shout out, Adamine! Adamine! If you is there on the nother side, let me in. That never work, so I call out, *Writer Man. Writer Man!* I shout it out, *Writer Man, come open this door and let me see what the hell you have done to me! What is it you write that I cannot see?* But he don't answer me because he was really gone for the day. He gone and the day start to lose its shape. Apocalypse begin. I feel the madness come back to split

170

me in two. And the place feel dark though I know, I know, I know that I was in a bright place. I know I could walk out right then and go into the streets. But it did feel to me like I was in a room again. A terrible room where the walls was soft and no light could get in. Water start run down my face because I feel the darkness pressing down on me, and the Saviour who was supposed to come and let me out of every goddam place they ever lock me up in wasn't there to let me out. And I did start to think, how the hell I reach here again? How I really reach back here? I had to put my hands on the side of my head to prevent every thought from slipping out and scattering. I had to start counting from one to whatever number I could manage to reach. I had to start saying my ABC. I had to say my mother's name. I had to say my own name. Whatever I know for a fact I just keep on saying that thing to steady my nerves. One, two, three, four. One, two, three, four, five. A, B, C, D, E, F, G. My mama's name was Pearline Portious. My husband's name was Milton Dehaney. My own name is Adamine Bustamante. Yes indeedy, my name is Adamine Bustamante and I did born amongst the lepers.

Shhhhhhhhh

Well hear me now, and study this lesson: every story have its own mind, its own opinion on things. And every story have its own legs; it can walk bout whenever it want. And every story have its own mouth, so it can talk, or else it can keep quiet. Hear that and understand this warning. If Mr Writer Man can lock his door then this story can lock its mouth. Let him continue with his make-up fairy tale, but let him continue without me, for I not

171

sharing one more word with him. If he want to carry on he will just have to find those who can offer their piece of the story. For nothing in this world happen by itself just so. Every story have its own witnesses, its Matthew, Mark, Luke and John.

Part Three

IN WHICH OTHERS BEAR WITNESS
TO THE STORY

The Husband

Milton Dehaney is a dishevelled man who lives in a dishevelled flat. While there has been some attempt to tidy up, a space cleared so that I can sit down, I can see that on most days he lives in a space which would kindly be called eclectic. Once I have wedged my way into the cleared space on the musty brown couch, he begins to talk straight away. I am almost thankful that there is no offer of tea or biscuits because I would be suspicious of anything unearthed from a cupboard in this flat. I am so busy fumbling to turn on the tape-recorder that I miss his first remarks, but it seems he is admitting that on the morning he met my mother, Adamine Bustamante, he was in rather a grumpy mood.

Everyone but him seemed glad to be at the airport that morning. It appeared that there were more smiles than faces to house those smiles, and all the faces were dark and glistening, as if oil had been rubbed on them. The air was thick with the sweet smell of cocoa butter, so thick that Milton scowled and wrinkled his fat nose. He, of course, does not tell me that his nose was fat, but I see that it is fat now and it was most likely fat then because a nose is one of those things that generally does not lose or gain weight.

'You could always depend on those people to shame you,' he tells me, 'because don't care how they travel far from their little no-name islands, they still take their ignorant and low-rated ways with them. They can't change.'

Ignorant and low-rated. It is an opinion he pronounces liberally,

175

applying it to many people, but most especially to my mother, who was the person he had gone to meet that morning. She was his wife-to-be. When she was finally delivered through the airport doors, toting her luggage behind her, Milton's heart fell, became a useless limp thing inside his chest. He had never laid eyes on her before but he recognise her with that fatalistic certainty that some people have – an expectation that life keeps on throwing up shit and that every situation will turn out for the worst. So this woman with the far-too-serious eyes, this unattractive and buffoonish-looking creature, was bound to be the one he was waiting on.

As he narrates the encounter, Milton does what I imagine he did then: he looks up at the ceiling and shakes his head. He describes her. She had the elaborate headtie of a Revivalist, a pair of scissors swinging from a rope around her waist, and three pencils stuck behind her ear. Her dress, he concedes, was spanking new, but this only served to highlight the crudeness of its stitching, the simplicity of its design, as if this woman had picked it up from some low-rated dressmaker that very morning. The light cotton material was of course inappropriate for the British weather.

Milton sighed but waved a dispirited hand in her direction as she approached.

The Revivalist woman looked at him briefly, and then walked on by with such determination that Milton felt a little silly, and then relieved. It wasn't her after all. Thank God. He turned his gaze back to the airport doors, which were steadily delivering more and more passengers onto England. Milton now allowed himself to hope that his new wife would be something like his previous wife, Doris.

Doris Dehaney had died the year before. She had always been a sickly woman, even when they had lived together in Jamaica. As Milton tells it, she had asthma; high blood pressure; low blood sugar; and she fainted regularly. There was almost nothing that poor Doris hadn't been afflicted with. After she had migrated to England, the eventual combination of hay fever in the summer, bronchitis in the autumn and influenza in the winter had been too much for her delicate system. Without much of a fight, she had succumbed.

Milton tells me unabashedly that while he had suspected it before, he knew for sure once Doris was gone that he was the kind of man who simply needed to have a wife. The small apartment he and Doris had lived in, the selfsame one in which I am now interviewing him, descended into chaos. It was as if he began to misplace bits of the structure − losing whole sections of its architecture. He lost the kitchen first. It was buried beneath pots and pans and a suffocating mountain of carrier bags and boxes of Chinese takeout he had begun to eat night after night. Then, judging by the squeaks, it was invaded by a family of mice. He lost the bedroom next. It was somewhere beneath a pile of clothes belonging to him and Doris. He had to sleep in the one remaining room, squashing his fat body into the bathtub each night. But soon enough he began to lose this room as well. Mildew and great tufts of mould began to colonise the space. After Milton was put on antibiotics for the second time, it was with resignation that he began to look for a new wife.

He fancied at first that he would trade up from Doris and marry an English woman. Indeed, he dated one for five weeks. Linda was many years his junior, fresh out of college, and would always say to him, 'You know, I have no problem being with a darkie. In fact, I think it's kind of thrilling.'

He didn't mind that she said this to him, but was uncomfortable when she insisted on saying it to just about everyone. She would tell waiters in restaurants, people out walking their dogs, and random commuters on the train. Her fingers defiantly intertwined with his, she would shout it to just about anyone who would listen, as if to advertise how utterly transgressive she was.

She was apparently the kind of girl who had learned too late the joy of rebellion, who now got a high from sticking it to the world, and who broke rules to feel more alive only because in her heart she was so repressed. So she said she had no problem being with a darkie, no problem at all, and she said it so often that soon Milton realised she meant the opposite.

One night she took him to meet her parents. At the end of the meal she helped her mother to clear the plates. The two women disappeared into the kitchen. Linda's father looked at Milton and Milton looked at the father. They smiled politely and nodded at each other but found nothing to say. They could hear the sound of dishes being scraped, and then the voices.

'You know, Mum, I don't care what you and Father think. I have no problem being with a darkie. In fact, it's kind of thrilling.'

'Yes, dear, but he is awfully old. He's almost our age.'

Linda made a sound. It seemed she was surprised and almost disappointed that their objection was not to Milton's colour. She tried to remind her mother.

'He is black, and I don't care.'

She needed her rebellion to matter.

'We don't have any problem with you being with a darkie but gosh, Linda, there are so many of them about, you might have chosen a better-looking one.'

When they came back out Linda looked at Milton as if for the first time, a new emotion narrowing her eyes and curling her lips. She didn't walk him to the door that evening, and that was that.

So Milton decided he was better off sending for a wife. Others had done it, requested a wife from back home – an Esme, or a Geraldine, or a Puncie – in much the same way as they asked for sugar or cigarettes or hard-dough bread to be sent. Milton wrote to Lucas Gilles, the Captain of a Revival band he had once been a part of, and Lucas wrote back promptly to say it was good to hear from a long-lost sheep, and that he in fact knew just the right helpmeet for Milton, and also that the church badly needed money for a new building and he would be grateful if he, Milton, could

178

donate a little something, living so prosperously as he no doubt did in England. So Milton scrimped and saved and sent money towards the Church Building Fund, and more money for a plane ticket for his wife-to-be. And this is how he ended up at the airport that morning, waiting for a fiancée he had never met.

One by one, the shiny smiling faces found their loved ones and left. Milton stood alone, feeling even more miserable, but then he felt a sensation in his back as though someone was staring at him. He turned around and saw her again, my mother. She was sitting on one of the airport benches observing him. Milton's misery transformed itself into pure anger. He stomped over.

'Woman, I really hope you don't name Adamine Bustamante, because any how you name Adamine Bustamante then we starting off on the wrong, wrong foot. You never see me wave at you earlier? You is blind or something?'

Adamine did not flinch. Instead she ran her eyes up and down this man she would be married to in less than twenty-four hours. Milton, I imagine, would have tried to suck in his gut and lift his head as high as possible. But my mother's eyes were all disapproval. She seemed as displeased with him as he was with her. Her first words to him:

'Them tell me you was supposed to be a mighty man of God. You don't look like that to me.'

'But excuse you!' Milton snapped. 'For somebody that coming straight from the dungle heap, you is quite facety! Try don't start with me, woman. Awoah!'

'Excuse me nothing.' Adamine spat.

('Right there on the airport floor!' Milton says to me incredulously. 'She spit!')

Adamine sucked her teeth and shook her head.

Milton hated her. He uses this word. Hate. For what the hell had she been expecting? What did a mighty man of God even look like? And how was it that she could make him feel so small, so quickly?

179

He does not tell me that he was clenching his fists that morning, but he is clenching them as he tells me this story, so I imagine that his body is also remembering the experience, and recreating it. I wonder then whether Adamine saw this, his fists, and whether she knew, as he did, that as bad as they both thought things were going to get, they would in fact work out a whole lot worse.

The Matron

I meet Sylvia Lightbourne in a home for the elderly. She is happy to see me because she doesn't often get visitors. I look on her and think she has become that kind of old that has finally erased all traces of its youth. But when she begins talking, there is, beneath the gravel of her voice, a kind of steel, and it is in this sound that she carries her past. So if I close my eyes and just listen, I can imagine her as someone else – as the matron she once was.

It was the 1970s, she tells me, and whenever she sat at the little brown desk in her little blue office at St Osmund's, she did so with a sigh. From that desk she had a front-row seat to one of the strangest and greatest wars of the twentieth century. Strange, because both sides in this altercation – the conservatives and the liberals – wanted the same bloody thing. Both were fighting to achieve similar ends, so it was like a tug-of-war with both teams pulling on the same end of the rope. The only people who were going to suffer were those caught, as the hospital was, slap bang in the middle.

Sylvia pulls her shawl a little closer around her and shivers. It occurs to me how much old people like to reminisce about wars.

There had been a time, she continues, when she had potted plants in her office, framed pictures of her two daughters, and a print of a Bellini Madonna on the wall. But when she had settled into the job, and saw the war that was being waged, she decided to bunker up. She took down the Bellini Madonna, took the potted plants and the framed pictures back to her house, and emptied the little office of its soul. Instead it became a sterile but functional place and, she admits, that suited her just fine. Even after she had been matron for seven years and counting, Sylvia Lightbourne still had in mind that it would all end soon.

The war was a simple one. Everyone wanted the mental hospital to close. Not just St Osmund's, but all of them. The Conservative Party felt that the hospitals had become too much of a strain on the budget. Hospitals were all well and good if patients got better and were discharged to live productive, taxpaying lives; but such was hardly ever the case with the mentally ill. For those who suffered the most chronic cases of schizophrenia, schizoaffective disorders, multiple personality disorders, manic depression; for those who heard voices in the walls and saw UFOs frisbeeing themselves across the sky each night; for those who became loud and aggressive if you simply looked at them too closely – treatment in a hospital added up to many, many thousands of pounds per month, a staggering figure when multiplied by the many months of a patient's life. The conservatives began to mutter that even the most generous of governments would rather spend its cash elsewhere.

And if the hospitals thought they were going to get support from the other side, they were wrong. A collection of pamphlets had begun circulating and a few Hollywood films had been made. Together they painted a grim picture – mental asylums that resembled little more than dungeons, places so grey and lifeless they could have featured in a Charles Dickens novel. Sylvia Lightbourne had read the pamphlets, had watched the films, and although she, more than anyone else, knew that these stories were exaggerated, a bending of the truth, she felt helpless. Her own two daughters would come over for Sunday dinner and eye her suspiciously.

'I just can't believe you subject people to shock therapy,' one had said weightily, as if she had just discovered her mother was working for the Nazis.

Sylvia had sighed, not knowing how to explain that in her

experience electrotherapy wasn't a bad thing, that it wasn't the random plugging of people into a wall socket. She had seen it help some of her worst patients – severely depressed psychopaths who had been fully intent on killing themselves and had shown no response to any other kind of therapy. Sylvia had seen them calm down dramatically and go on to live healthier, happier lives. But she knew that a great wave was building against the institution for which she worked.

There were petitions. And then a mob marched to Downing Street, a loud rabble of the sane and the not-so-sane, a large, riotous group mumbling, muttering, chanting and waving placards, PSYCHIATRY KILLS, LOVE IS BETTER THAN SHOCK! It made for good TV and sensational headlines.

Sylvia recognised the sentiment that was growing. It was a passion that was essential to every crusade – the passion of a people who had finally found something to believe in, to fight for, and in doing so invest their lives with worth. Their worthiness was directly proportional to the worthlessness of what they were fighting against.

There was no way of winning this war. And so this is why, whenever she went to her soulless office at St Osmund's and sat at her desk, she did so with a sigh, knowing the end would be coming soon.

The Gardener

Mrs Evelyn Young had loved her son with that special, blinding kind of love that women lavish on boys who are the only mementos they have left of a man swallowed and lost in the belly of war. It was a dangerous kind of love – one that tied up a young boy in its apron strings, covered him with an emotion so fierce and complex it was as good as locking him in an oven, turning it on high, and expecting the child to come out undamaged. Evelyn Young's son was, in a word, fucked. Bruce Young resented the strength of his mother's affection, a thing so huge he would never be able to reciprocate. He gave up trying soon enough and decided instead that he would dislike the woman. But whereas his mother's love was sharp and penetrating, his dislike was blunt and wide and ever expanding.

He wasn't close to anyone in the village either, so his dislike grew to include them all. He crinkled his nose whenever Mr Williams, the pig farmer, was near by; he did the same around Mrs Devonish, who didn't need to raise pigs to smell funny; he shielded his eyes against the glare of Mrs Jones's badly dyed hair; and he kept his distance from Mr Jones, who it was said used to bugger his sheep on occasion. And because such things – foul-smelling people, bad hair dye, and the occasional rape of sheep – were usual enough occurrences in every village, the people began to wonder about the boy. The villagers became wary when no matter how kindly they said *hallo there*, or how they stooped down on their

184

knees and smiled at him, or how they pinched his cheek or ruffled his hair, he would only ever stare back at them contemptuously. One could say, however, that his relationship with the community was, in the end, healthier than his relationship with his mother, for at least with the community, emotions were exchanged measure for measure, and any wariness towards him was a direct reflection of his aloofness towards them.

Then his mother died. The boy was fifteen at the time. She had put her nose right up to a bluebell, taken a deep inhale as if she were trying to drink in the pollen, and a disturbed bee had flown straight up into her nose. There is no account of this actual moment, but it is widely imagined that Evelyn Young would have yelped. Bruce, it is imagined, would have looked up in surprise, and then, something unexpected. He would have giggled. Mrs Young's face turned red. Hives came up all over her body. She looked at her son with astonished eyes and tried to make a sound. She began fanning her face desperately as it turned from red to blue. She shook her head from side to side as if that would open the airways and allow her to breathe again. Her whole face swelled to an extraordinary size. She collapsed into the mud and all the while, Bruce just watched.

The next morning it was as if a wet carpet had been spread over the village. Everyone wrinkled their nose, but no one bothered to ask what the smell was. The following day it was more obvious, the smell more alive, and people now recognised it as the sweet choking smell of something rotting. On the third day the smell was so rank that many couldn't swallow their breakfast, and they could now tell it was coming from the Youngs' house. They went over and knocked on the door, wanting to know whether a dog or sheep had died.

There was no answer. Only then did someone say, 'Has anyone seen Evelyn these past three days? Anyone?'

There was a moment of silence, and then they banged on the

185

door even harder, more desperately, as if time were suddenly of the essence, as if they could break in and save her life. They had to call the police.

Three constables broke down the door, and the village crowded in behind them, handkerchiefs clamped firmly over their noses. They were not prepared for what they saw and would have nightmares about it for years to come. It was not only the sight of Mrs Young, dead as a doornail in her courtyard garden, her face swollen and black and already beginning to rot. It was the boy as well. He was still there working, stepping over and around his mam's body as if it were just a bag of rubbish. And also it was the garden itself. The most beautiful garden any of the villagers had seen. There were bluebells and foxgloves and marigolds all laid out in their own circles and squares. They knew Mrs Young had had a black finger. The running joke was that she couldn't even grow weeds. So it was this brooding, dislikable boy who had grown these flowers, who had arranged them in their patterns, this boy who had left his mother to rot in the middle of all his work, as if this was the only thing she was good for – plant food.

Fifteen years old, and they took him out in handcuffs as if he were his own man. But the coroner soon found the bee in Mrs Young's nose, and a forensic analysis determined she had died from a massive allergic reaction. Still, the villagers would never understand why Bruce had not called a doctor, or an ambulance, or the police. Why had he just left his own mam there, dead and rotting, and carried on as if it were nothing? They answered this question for themselves. It was because the boy was evil.

Even the parson's wife whispered, 'Pardon me, but that boy is one sick fucker.'

I know that the pastor's wife whispered this because she is the one I meet years later and she repeats this very thing.

Bruce Young was passed from hand to hand after that – two months here, two months there. He was at that awkward age where it would do no good to settle him in a foster house. Finally, on his seventeenth birthday he went back to the village and lived in his mother's house for a year before selling it and disappearing for good.

Now a nonegarian, the pastor's wife has become the pastor's widow, and she tells me, 'We heard he ended up at St Osmund's after that. You know the one – the nuthouse. We was all relieved when we heard that, we was. We said, well he finally ended up where he belonged. But would you believe it, he didn't go there as no patient. Oh no. Fellow just wandered onto the grounds and started tending their gardens, and before long, that sick fucker had got himself a job!'

The Husband

The first words exchanged between Milton and Adamine were, of course, not pleasant, and this began a pattern. They fought about everything. There was the matter of her name. On the way home from the airport Milton had glanced into her passport.

'I thought your name was Adamine Bustamante?'

'It is.'

'But it say Pearline Portious right here. What happen? Is you cannot read?'

'I can read very well, thank you, sir.'

'Well I suppose I can call you anything I want. I can just call you Daisy Cowshit for all you care.'

He didn't tell her that what he was really upset about was the fact that he had already set an appointment at the register office for himself and 'Adamine Bustamante'. He imagined he would look like an idiot in the morning, having to correct his fiancée's name. What kind of marriage was this going to be when he didn't even know the name of his bride?

It was her turn to explode when she saw the flat. Milton hadn't cleared away anything. When he opened the door, Adamine staggered back at the smell, and when the light was switched on she began to unleash such a string of curses that had she been in Jamaica, where people were still charged for indecent language, she would have been broke after five minutes. Adamine went on for an hour. Milton was properly scared. He tried to calm her. He begged her to think of the neighbours. He explained that this was no way to behave in England. She told him to kiss his bumboclawt. She demanded to be sent back home to Jamaica because she wasn't coming to live in this, no way. Milton, ashamed, began sheepishly to put things in order. Thankfully, Adamine's anger became a vigorous dusting and wiping and sweeping and throwing of things into the hall, where Milton had simply to catch them and take them down to the bin before the neighbours noticed.

Milton admits he should have been grateful for this at least. But the next morning it was his turn again. This time it was the matter of her clothes. When she woke up and started to get ready to go to the register office with him, she began by wrapping her head.

'What wrong? Your skull crack?' he remarked. 'Your forehead bleeding? You have migraine?'

'What is it now, Mr Milton? What now?'

'But just look on you eeh!' He grimaced, 'From you step out of that airport yesterday everybody been looking on you. You will have to learn fast, woman. You can't wear them kind of things in England. Them will think you is backward or something.'

'What wrong with what I wearing? We is not Revivalists? Is not this what we always wear?'

Milton shook his head violently.

'No no no, darling. Not in England. You will have to find yourself a proper hat if you want to go to church. As for me, I stop go to them jump-up church. They not civilised. You ever see the queen wrapping her head up in foolishness, falling on floor and all them kind of bush-nigger stupidness? You ever see the queen swinging a cutlass in the spirit?'

'I don't business bout no queen. What queen have to do with who we is? I worship God ...'

'Too much talk! Too much talk! I just can't abide a woman with so much mouth.'

189

'Listen to me, man. I don't pay taxes fi mi mouth, so I can say what I bloody well want when I want to say it.'

For the second time Milton clenched his fists and this time he made sure that Adamine saw them.

'I bet you can't say anything when your lips is cut in two and swell up, though.'

'Oh! Oh! I see now. Is threaten you come to threaten me? But you know that is Father God pickney you threatening? Well then ... box me! Box me if you think you is badder than God.'

She didn't expect it. Milton tells me that he didn't expect it either. But all the same, he hit her. Straight across the face. The sound was as sharp as lightning. And truth be told, he was sorry that he did it. Not sorry for hitting her, he quickly explains, for he is the kind of man who apparently believes some women need an occasional roughing up or else they just won't conform. Even Doris had received a good slap now and then. But Milton was sorry for what he saw happen in Adamine's eyes, something that diminished before him, as if a light had suddenly been switched off. It was as if she had lost her faith in God right then and there – her God who could not defend her from this slap.

He remembered how, when he first came to this country, his faith had been all that he had, the only thing he could lean on, the only buffer he had against all that was thrown at him. It had taken him a long while to lose that faith, and when he did, he had done so on his own. No one had taken it from him. But Adamine seemed to lose hers in just a moment and he was sorry that he was the one who had taken it from her.

190

The Gardener

For all of my research, for all the drawers I have pulled out and rifled through, for all the hundreds of files I have turned over and over, for all the rooms and houses and hospitals I have gone back to and stood in and tried simply to feel their history, to reach out to the ghosts of that space, for all of the terrible past that I have dug up like a dog anxiously uncovering a fresh skeleton, for all of this I have not yet been able to find a clear photograph of Bruce Young. Always this silent, brooding, flower-loving rapist is turning his back, is ducking under someone's arms, or is lost in the blur of his own movement. It is as if the world wants there to be no evidence of the man's existence.

But then, I am here. I exist. That is evidence enough.

To describe him I must therefore do an imprecise kind of science. I look closely at Adamine. She has not spoken to me for days, and yet there is something she can tell me even in her silence. I can look for myself in her. I must decide which parts of me she is responsible for.

I take note of her lips. I definitely have her lips. And also her tiny slits of eyes. And the texture that prevents my hair from ever being straight comes from her own lovely afro. Of course I tan easily, the sun always drawing out from my skin the deposit of melanin that hides under the surface. I have her cheekbones too, and most embarrassingly, her behind. I have grown up into this strange mixed-up mulatto man with a black woman's behind, broad and high, filling out my trousers.

I catalogue each of these things and whatever is left, whichever part of me I cannot find in Adamine, I ascribe instead, however inaccurately, to Bruce Young. So I imagine him as tall, and his eyes as green, and his teeth as imperfect, a wide space between his two front incisors. He is Caucasian, of course – that much is obvious even in the blurred photographs. But I think he must have been desperately, desperately Caucasian, so that when the sun does not draw out my deposit of melanin, people have often confused me as white, and even on the days when I am my darkest self, they think that perhaps I am simply Mediterranean. I imagine Bruce Young was pudgy around the mid-section, just as I have always been. That he had long, skinny legs and big knees. Adamine would have felt those knees pressed into her sides, the clammy flatness of his hands covering her mouth.

There are days when I like to imagine that once or twice she may have bit down hard enough to pierce his skin and taste the salt of his O-positive blood. I would like to believe this, that even in a small way, Adamine might have scarred my father, Bruce Young.

The Nurse

When I meet Julie Astwood and remark on the size of her office, she explains that she recently qualified to be a nurse practitioner, as if this should make everything clear. It takes a while, but I eventually understand that this position is much more senior than being a nurse, or even a matron. On the wall it says that Julie Astwood has just received her DNP – a Doctorate of Nursing Practice. So she is a nurse who is called Doctor. I am confused again, but I decide this is not what I have come to ask about. I want to know about a time, long ago, when she was still simply a nurse. A psychiatric nurse.

I relax in her presence, for Julie has an open face and a kind manner. To get things going I ask her, how did you get into nursing?

She laughs so hard the table between us shakes. I raise my eyebrows.

'It's a hell of a story,' she warns, 'but I'm no longer embarrassed to tell it.'

So she tells me.

Things changed on the day that Marcus Ramsay insisted on putting his fingers inside Julie's knickers. She was sixteen, and she knew that nothing good would come of this. Such clear insight had bypassed her three older sisters, who had been beautiful girls, but had now become a trinity of overweight mothers, living on the dole, and taking it in turns to look after her. Julie's own mother

193

had said she was due a permanent break from mothering because she was still in her forties for fuck's sake and she needed to live something of her life before it was over.

Julie's three sisters had each had their own knickers violated by a boy in secondary school and they repeated these stories, competing to see who had the cutest boy and which one had the cleverest fingers. They swooned over these memories of the star footballer, the ace cricketer, the fit skinny lad – and how they had given themselves to him willingly and wouldn't hesitate to do so again.

But Julie, having observed her sisters and the non-eventful lives they led, pinpointed this moment as a kind of death. The day a boy puts his fingers inside you and you let him, she decided, was the day a girl resigned herself to the most banal of existences. She wasn't going to let that happen. So when, after class was let out one Thursday, Marcus Ramsay held her back (as he often did) but this time began to put his fingers inside her knickers, Julie Astwood understood the moment. She had prepared herself for this moment. She had to make a decision.

What she hadn't known, however, was that when those fingers reached inside her pants, she would want them to stay there.

She blushes when she tells me this, that she hadn't counted on that wetness spreading from inside her. The body betrays you, she says, and I was sixteen.

Julie had to close her eyes, imagine her sisters, imagine their lives as her own, before she grasped Marcus's wrist tightly.

'No, stop.'

Unlike Julie, Marcus Ramsay did not have any older siblings to learn lessons from. He didn't understand the pattern of life she wanted to escape; he didn't know why her hand was suddenly stopping his. It annoyed him. All he seemed to understand was that he was already six feet tall, that his torso was toned and whenever he scored a goal and tore off his shirt everyone looked at him impressed. He understood that he had an impressive knob that

194

bobbed up and down in his shorts, and this made both girls and boys ogle him even more; he understood that Julie, skinny as she was, was the fittest bird in class, with her long brown hair and pointy little nose and her tits like small melons; he understood that this was what they were supposed to be doing, getting hot and heavy in the classroom, making everyone jealous, not only because they wanted to, but because that's just how things went, it was the script.

Julie pushed him away as he tried to force his hand.

'No, Marcus. I really mean it.'

'What do you mean, no?' he stammered.

It could have been an honest question. The boy simply didn't understand why they shouldn't be doing what everyone wanted them to do, and what they wanted to do themselves. And maybe, Julie concedes, if she had found a way to tell him, *because we can be more than this, because this will condemn us to a life we're better than,* he would have tried to see things her way. But all Julie knew how to say then was, 'Fuck off!'

Marcus's hands were suddenly on her breasts squeezing them harder than they'd ever been squeezed before. She started whimpering. And Marcus, she swears, was suddenly more turned on. He had stumbled, as it were, into a fetish. But it would only last sixty seconds. His dick was rock solid. (60) 'You fuck off!' he growled (50) in a voice he had never used before, holding her awkwardly with one hand, (40) unfastening his trousers with the other, (30) his trousers which fell into a puddle around his ankles. (20) He shoved Julie to the floor, (10) freed himself and pushed his hardness into her mouth. (0).

That was the end of his fetish. In an instant he was suddenly screaming, hollering, doubled over on the floor, while Julie, her mouth full of blood, was running away, a piece of foreskin between her teeth.

Julie leans over to tell me how, in a school, some stories never

195

die, and this was one of them. Julie Astwood taking a proper munch off Marcus Ramsay's dick. Long after students had graduated, after they had forgotten the name 'Julie Astwood', they would still remember the incident and the other names by which they called her. Knob-biter. Cock-muncher. Circumciser. Miss Meany Guillotiney.

At first, Julie was distraught but then she discovered something she might not have otherwise. Without the distraction of boys – they naturally avoided her now – or of being popular, she wasn't a bad student after all. It was as if, having learnt one lesson, others cued up at the side of her head trying to enter this one willing mind that could make room for them.

It was a pity, Julie tells me, that she hadn't discovered this latent potential sooner. If she had had even another year of school she might have got into Cambridge or Oxford. Still, she managed to leave school with better grades than anyone had expected, certainly better than any of her sisters. She went on to nursing school and from there she went to St Osmund's where she met my mother, Adamine.

She comes around to hold my hand when she says, smiling, 'I will always remember your mother, because of how she came to St Osmund's.'

The Husband

Milton lowers his eyes and says he is about to tell me something personal, and that I must promise not to repeat it, because it is not the kind of thing a man likes to say. So I lie to him. I say no, I will not repeat it. And it is true, I will not say it to anyone. But I will write it. So this is how I find out the most curious thing about the marriage of Milton and Adamine.

They did everything a husband and wife do together. They ate together. They argued with each other. They slept in the same bed. But they never had sex.

Three years of living in the same tiny space – the bedroom, kitchen and bathroom – and still the marriage was never consummated. Some nights she was the one tugging at his shorts, trying to find life there, but he was never interested and would turn over in the bed. It was this that Adamine threw at Milton one Saturday.

Saturdays were Milton's letter-writing day. He had his special paper and his ballpoint pens and he would sit down and compose letters to his mama, his cousin Tunki, and any number of people back home. He was proud of these letters and even harboured the thought that one day they would make him famous. For this reason he diligently wrote each letter twice and kept a copy. He shows me some of them, because I am a writer, and waits for my approval. I smile and say lovely, but of course they aren't very good.

On this particular Saturday, Adamine was in a singing mood. She sang this song and then that song and every song scattered Milton's thoughts. After an hour he found himself still looking at a blank piece of paper.

'Please, Ada, for godsake. I trying to do mi letter-writing.'

'How a little praise song to stop you from writing your letter? How you so fenkeh-fenkeh so?'

'Just cool it, Adamine. Just give me a little peace here.'

She wasn't in a mood to give in.

'The Apostle Paul write the most beautiful letters to the Church in Corinthians when him was in jail and him must have had plenty distractions round him.'

'I am not the fucking Apostle Paul!' Milton shouted.

'You damn right bout that.'

He shook his head and turned back to his paper. Soon Adamine was singing again. He stood up. 'Adamine, I really don't want to do it, but if you provoke me in here today, God help you!'

She did then what he had never seen her do before. She stood up tall and put her face against his raised fist.

'Come do it. Do it, Son of Man. For that is the only part of you that have strength for a woman. Your man-parts soft and can't do a goddam thing. So may as well you hit me.'

He fell back into his chair, realising for the first time that her God had not died after all; He had simply been hiding in a corner of her mind, waiting to ambush him.

The Nurse

Julie Astwood is laughing when she tells me there probably should have been a whole course in Nursing School devoted to the business of keys. This was her main assignment at St Osmund's: not monitoring the treatment of patients, not assessing new residents, not intervening in the many crises that happened each day. Rather, she was the person put in charge of keys. She always needed to remember which ones went into which doors. She carried around a large bunch, a jangly metal pom-pom of bit keys, barrel keys, skeleton keys and more. Almost every door within St Osmund's was kept locked and walking the short distance of a hundred yards could potentially involve the unlocking and relocking of half a dozen.

Julie considered it something of a marathon whenever she had to walk from her ward to the front door to collect a new patient. On these occasions she had to pass through a total of fourteen doors. On these journeys, she always tried to guess what kind of patient the asylum would be getting and the unlocking of the final front door became, for her, something like the unwrapping of a gift.

Julie remembers every patient she opened the door to, but she recalls none so clearly as my mother – a bundle of red and white cloth collapsed on her head and falling like rags over her face.

Julie smiled encouragingly.

'Why hello there. Welcome to St Osmund's.'

Adamine didn't respond, but Julie remembers her eyes. She tells

199

me she had eyes that could make you feel as if you were falling.

Julie led her to the ward, a long corridor that smelt faintly of piss. A line of twenty-two cots ran the length of it and the cot assigned to my mother was at the very end. Julie began to make introductions to the frazzle-haired women in their nightgowns as she walked down the line. She had always found this to be good practice.

'Pearline, this is Maud. Maud, this is Pearline.'

But my mother stopped her after this first introduction.

'I know all of these women already. Them is lepers. I finally come back to my own people. And another thing, my name is not Pearline. It is Adamine Bustamante. Please learn that.'

The Matron

Sylvia Lightbourne has stopped talking. Instead, she is observing a woman across the room who is sitting in a chair and looking out at nothing in particular. She whispers to me without turning away her eyes, 'Two days. Three at most.'

Then she looks up and says in a lazy way, 'It's a skill you learn in a place like this; you look into people's eyes and you can tell how much time they have left. That's why we don't look in mirrors at my age. None of us do. We're too afraid we'll see our own time, and we know it won't be long.'

She tells me she was able to do a similar kind of thing at St Osmund's, make a quick diagnosis of a patient just by looking into his or her eyes.

'There was nothing official about these evaluations. You didn't share them with anyone, mind you, but everyone who works in a mental hospital does it, and the longer you've worked there, the more on the money your guesses are likely to be. So listen to me when I tell you, Pearline Portious-Dehaney was one of the most serious cases that ever walked through those doors.'

Why? I ask. Why was her craziness so special?

Sylvia Lightbourne shrugs. 'It wasn't just that Pearline lived in her own world, young man – she was the kind who could take you into that world with her. I wouldn't say her madness was contagious. I wouldn't put it like that. But maybe ... maybe it was evangelical.'

201

She tells me then of their first meeting. A young nurse, Julie Astwood, had brought Pearline up to her office on the first day. This was standard practice.

'Well, who do we have here?' Sylvia had said, smiling as she opened a file. 'Mrs Pearline Portious-Dehaney, eh?'

'My name is Adamine Bustamante,' my mother snapped.

Sylvia shook her head slowly, carefully. She eased herself up from behind her little desk, went around it and sat beside my mother. She took her black hands into her own and said, 'Now, now, Pearline. You're here to get better, and we're here to help you get better. So this won't do at all. You'll meet all kinds of people here at St Osmund's who will tell you they are anyone and everyone – from Jesus Christ, to the Pope, to Elvis Presley, to King George. Well now, all that nonsense doesn't do anyone any good, does it? Best you just be yourself, eh, Pearline? Do we have a deal? In no time at all you will be back with your husband. Wouldn't you like that?'

Sylvia Lightbourne tries to describe my mother's eyes to me, and how she had the distinct impression that she was suddenly the one being evaluated. Adamine sucked her teeth.

'My name is Adamine Bustamante,' she said again, and her tone was final.

Sylvia deliberately and carefully, frowned. She returned to her position behind the desk.

'You will find, Mrs Portious-Dehaney, that the days and weeks here have a very strict order. This is to help you. You will try not to fall out of line. You will be happy to know that Wednesday nights are film nights, if you are well behaved of course. And Sunday is for church. I trust you are fully continent, Mrs Portious-Dehaney? That we won't be having to put you on the wet and dirty ward? Good, good. Now off with you.'

202

The Husband

Milton Dehaney continues.

'After that I don't lay a hand on her again, cause I realise she don't take disciplining. I just make her have her own way in things, for I understand too that she was one dangerous bitch. So she start to wrap up her head again. I never say nothing. She start to walk out into the city. I never say kemps. She start to go out into the heart of Birmingham, and Lord have mercy on all of we, that mad woman say she gone there to give warning. The whole time I just keep my own counsel. I make the cards fall where they may.'

But on the night my mother did not return, Milton tells me he was surprised by how worried he was. He imagined the worst, that maybe she had been held; maybe she had been raped; killed; left for dead in a back alley; or maybe she had fallen sick in the street and was now in the hospital; or maybe a lorry had run over her. But as surprised as he was by this first reaction, he was equally ashamed of the second.

For Milton felt a sense of relief. And then it became something more than relief. Soon it bordered on a wish. He hoped that something truly tragic had befallen Adamine. He wondered what to do, and finally decided to do nothing. Still, he went to bed smiling. Milton decided he was going to call the police in the morning, but for just one night, one blessed night, he would enjoy being alone.

He slept more peacefully than he had in three years, but before the sun had come up there was a loud rapping at the front door. He dragged himself out of bed and opened the door to two grave-looking police officers.

They clasped their hats to their chests and Milton tried to frown and look worried.

'I'm sorry, Mr Dehaney, but we have bad news for you.'

Milton wondered then whether he could find it in his heart to bawl and carry on when they told him that his wife was dead. He hadn't even done as much for Doris, whom he truly missed. When Doris died he understood what widows and widowers meant when they said they had lost a part of themselves. But still, he had not been able to weep. He was so wrapped up in thinking about how to react appropriately to Adamine's death that he barely heard the police officers.

'We are sorry, Mr Dehaney, but your wife isn't well. We've been holding her for examination.'

When the words registered, Milton's heart sank. She was alive after all.

'Oh no. Oh Lord,' he said, genuinely heart-broken.

The officers patted his shoulders and explained where Adamine was. Milton told them thanks.

He was later called to testify on his wife's behalf. He was glad she wasn't in the room. He knew that he would not have been able to look her in the eyes as he told the doctor and the lawyers that his wife had been sick for a long, long time. Deranged. Crazy. He told them he was at his wits' end. He told them he would be much obliged if they took her away to a hospital where she could get proper treatment. He was willing to sign any paper to that effect.

And so Milton signed the papers and for him it was as if he were signing for a divorce.

The Nurse

By any standard the garden at St Osmund's was a thing of wonder. Julie tells me she had never before, and has never since, smelled anything so intoxicating or seen anything laid out so beautifully. Such intricate patterns. Such a perfect co-ordination of colours. It was a perfect place to escape from the choking asylum smell, that combination of piss, paraldehyde, carbolic soap, floor polish and boiled cabbage.

She knew who was responsible for this oasis. It was one of the male attendants, although she thought of him only as the gardener. When she speaks of him, this is what she calls him. The Gardener. He was a tall, lanky, gap-toothed man and she often saw him out there, either by himself or co-ordinating a group of patients. His voice was an incoherent mumble, and he had to resort to a kind of sign language. *Clip this leaf. Turn up that bit of soil. Water here.* Soon enough the patients would pick up on what he was saying. In fact, they seemed to relish their time out in the sun.

But Julie had an instant dislike for the man. At first, she felt guilty about this. Surely anyone capable of creating something as breathtaking as the garden couldn't be a bad person? But she trusted her instincts. There was something cold about Bruce Young, and she found herself trying to look into his eyes. She was never able to do this because she always found that he was staring straight back at her and she would feel a coldness spreading inside. Still, she thought, if only she could look at him once when he was relaxed, look at him in the way she had learned to look at her patients, she might be able to determine just how crazy the man really was.

The Husband

Milton admits he had to look up the word 'conjugal' when they assured him he would have conjugal rights. For the life of him, he couldn't work out what they were suggesting he do on any evening between the hours of 7 and 9 p.m. if he was in the mood. He tells me he laughed when he found out, and yet (he leans forward seriously) it was curious – when Adamine left he suddenly found his nature. That's how he puts it. He found his nature.

'Yes, my boy, I find it again. Strong, strong.'

He says no more but I have an unfortunate image of this old man with a raging erection, masturbating furiously, his free hand holding any garment that had once belonged to Adamine. I imagine that he would cum magnificently, gritting his teeth and whispering, 'Oh Lord, oh Lord!' and then wipe up the mess with one of her red and white headwraps.

But what Milton tells me is that he did not think of my mother again, this woman who had lived with him for three years. He was determined to erase her from his life.

Now that I am sitting in front of him, in this flat which has slipped back into a chaos it will never escape from again, he tells me, 'Young man, is only sake of the fact that you come here this morning and bring up her name that I even remembering these stories. It was a long time ago, three years in my life that never should have happened. And you know what? Whenever I have a form to fill out these days, I write down that I is single. Or else

I write that I is a widower. And I don't do it to be badmind. Is just that I truly forget about Ada. You ask if I even know where she is, but how I would know such a thing? She probably still in some madhouse or other. She probably even dead. I really couldn't care less.'

The Gardener

I now have a theory as to why there are no clear pictures of Bruce Young. It has something to do with the reason a microphone, for instance, will hum or squeak in the presence of a radio or a telephone. Something to do with waves, interference, the invisible, cosmic clashing of alike things. Maybe, whenever a camera's lens was trained on Bruce Young, he would stare right back at it and the thing would short-circuit.

He was a man who stared, who could stare comfortably for hours. And even if the person he was staring at was discomforted by the intensity of his gaze, he wouldn't stop. He freaked people out. Even dogs that came up to him growling would whimper and walk away, frightened by the scorch of his eyes.

On the day that my mother sat to eat her first meal at St Osmund's, his gaze was trained on her. Adamine looked up and then diverted her eyes. She concentrated instead on the green peas on her plate, and on the plate itself, and on her fork. But Bruce's gaze had already done its damage. She was aware of him. She started shivering and then began to pat her shoulders. She did it softly at first, but her movements soon began to grow. They became larger and larger and then it spread. A wave of nervousness was now going around the dining room, people suddenly mumbling to themselves and twitching, and at the centre of it all was Adamine. She was in her own storm, her hands no longer patting, but hitting her shoulders violently. It seemed as though she were shooing an invisible swarm of flies.

Bruce Young kept studying her.

A nurse ran over and insisted that Adamine calm down at once. Attendants went over with straps and held her but Adamine wriggled out of their grasps. She lifted her head and now she too stared across the room, matching Bruce Young, eye for eye, gaze for gaze. She pointed at him and bellowed, 'See him there and know his name, my people. Him is the one who name Abaddon. Him name is Rutibel. Some call him The Wicked One. Know his name, my people. Is him that name Satan.'

Bruce Young's mouth cracked into a gap-toothed smile as the attendants finally managed to restrain Adamine.

The Matron

Sylvia Lightbourne tells me that there were days when she felt that if retirement came the following morning, it wouldn't have come too soon. She was tired of it all. If she wasn't being accused by the protesters who had now started to picket outside the gates, she was sorting through complaints from her own staff.

There was this one nurse, she tells me conspiratorially, Julie Astwood, who was a particular pain.

'Oh,' she sighs, shaking her head. 'Oh,' she sighs again, 'that young woman was dead set against one of the male attendants. Every week it was a new complaint. Now it wasn't that I didn't believe her, but let me tell you, thirty years I'd worked in hospitals. Thirty years. And I knew a thing or two about how the damn place worked. And let me tell you, one doesn't get very far by investigating every indiscretion … Sometimes you have to let things slide.'

I try not to look surprised.

'Look, remember those were not good days. The protesters were right outside and they wanted a story, they wanted blood. And I sure as hell wasn't going to give them something they could use to shut us down for good.'

But even with all that said, Sylvia was truly perplexed by one of Nurse Astwood's gripes.

'She complained that the man had been giving some of the patients flowers. Flowers? I asked her. Yes, she tells me. Flowers. Well bloody hell,' and now Sylvia is smiling, 'if news like that had

211

leaked out we might actually have had a chance of staying open a while longer. But no, this nurse tells me. It wasn't just that he gave them flowers, but that he gave particular flowers to particular patients. You understand? So maybe he would give ivy blossoms to one, and daisies to another, and marigolds to another and so on and so forth. Never mixed it up. This is what the nurse tells me. Always the same flowers to the same people. Even I can admit it seemed a little psychotic.'

I have already heard the story about the flowers, so I try to keep the anger from creeping into my voice when I ask, 'But it wasn't just flowers, was it? Nurse Astwood was right to be suspicious. When you think of how it all ended, shouldn't you have listened to her?'

Sylvia bites her lips and her body begins to shake an old woman's shake. She purses her lips and her voice snaps out like a whip.

'What the hell was I to do? Let me tell you something about mental hospitals, young man. They mostly hire two kinds of persons – either those who would have been better suited as prison wardens, or those who would be better off as patients. Madness attracts madness. Simple as that. So fine, fine, the fellow and his flowers may not have been altogether here ...'

'But he was abusing patients!' I interject, but Sylvia continues speaking over me.

'... but if his only fault was that he gave flowers, blinking flowers, to a few of the patients then ... then I could certainly live with that.'

I wait for her body to stop shaking before I say, 'But that wasn't his only fault, was it? Are you able to live with that?'

'You're damned right I can.'

The Nurse

For the first time Julie's face is not open. Her eyes have become distant, as if she is looking at something far off, and cold, as if she is steeling herself. Without looking at me, she says, 'I believe he was ... I believe he was hurting them. Those patients he gave flowers to; those were the ones he hurt.'

'And Adamine?' I can't help but ask.

She nods. 'Yes. He always gave her flowers.'

The Gardener

I have been back to St Osmund's. It is, after all, the place where I first died. I have always felt this was an odd way to have entered the world, to have died first, and then to have revived. But then neither of these facts — that I was born, or that I died there — makes me unique.

I found this out because I have been through the records. There were other patients who delivered babies at the asylum. Magical babies. Immaculately conceived. There is never any mention of a father. I may not be able to prove that Bruce Young, behind his strange trail of daisies and petunias, impregnated each of these women; but I have listened to stories, and stories, and stories, and I am certain. I feel related to each child who was born at St Osmund's; I consider them my siblings. And in the same way, I feel related to everyone who died there. This is why I have been back, because it was as if I were returning to a family home.

The hospital remained empty for years after it was closed, as if it too had to take a moment to consider itself. Later it reopened as a hostel, so on the day that I returned and walked through the grounds, I was aware that things would have changed. This St Osmund's did not resemble the place I had read or heard about. There was too much light, too many open doors. And there was no garden.

It is the garden that I had wanted especially to see, the arrangement of flowers. But these too have slipped into the past and I am only able to imagine what it must have been like. I wonder whether Bruce Young gave his victims their flowers before, or after; was it a promise of something to come, or an apology for what he had done? And which specific flower did he give to my mother?

The Nurse

Julie knew that her complaints were not going to go anywhere. There were too many other things to worry about. The hospital was understaffed; they were short of medication; fights were always erupting; and she had noticed this business of the flowers and complained about it at the worst time of the year — the beginning of Suicide Season.

Whenever winter reached its end and outside began to defrost, and the bees and the daffodils and the birds came, it signalled the beginning of the hardest season for a mental hospital. In the spring patients would suddenly climb up to the roof and jump, or hang themselves by their pyjamas, or steal matches and set themselves on fire, or break glasses and plunge the jagged ends into their wrists, or try to escape the grounds and step in front of cars. Some came up with the most ingenious attempts, and if it weren't all so tragic one would want to congratulate them for their focus and creativity.

A good week was any one that ran its course without a hearse pulling up, an undertaker being called in, a body bag being dragged out. Julie understood that no one was going to listen to a complaint about an attendant who gave out flowers.

Even she herself hadn't thought it was *rape* at first. But then she noticed the way the patients acted around him. There was a subtle change in their bodies whenever Bruce Young handed them flowers. Julie noticed that they would flinch.

216

But if she had said this to Matron Lightbourne, the woman would have baulked.

'Flinched? Nurse Astwood, may I remind you that this is a mental hospital.'

It was true. Patients were not known for their fluid or graceful movements. They walked slowly. They looked around furtively. Their eyes blinked rapidly. And every so often a wave of nervousness passed through their bodies and they would flinch. To work in a mental hospital was to get used to occasional jerks and shivers, to people who for no apparent reason would lose control of their muscles at random moments.

Julie pauses, and then as if to change the subject, she tells me how she became aware of my existence. She had helped Adamine to the toilet one morning, and then the morning after that, and the morning after that. It was on the third morning that Julie placed her hand on the hollow of Adamine's back as she retched into the toilet, and asked quietly, 'Who did this to you, Ada?'

Adamine began to shake, weeping into the bowl.

'Who?' Julie asked again, her question as soft as her hand.

Adamine was gasping for air.

'Tell me who, Ada.'

'Satan,' Adamine, the Warner Woman, my mother, said at last. 'Is Satan who do it!'

Part Four

IN WHICH THE STORY INVENTS PARABLES,
AND SPEAKS A BENEDICTION
AND THEN ENDS

an instalment of a testimony spoken to the wind

Shhhhhhhhh

MAYBE SOMETIMES YOU have to tell a story crossways, because to tell it straight would ongly mean that it go straight by the person's ears who it intend for. For consider the words of Jesus: when the blessed Saviour go up on the mountain him did decide to speak in parables. He never just tell them that all of them was heathens, and that not a one of them could reach Heaven without him. Instead he talk bout hard ground and soft ground and ground that was full of macka and thorns, and how the seeds would grow according to what ground them did fall on; he talk bout the old woman who lose her coin and then find it again; him talk bout camels that cannot fit through the eye of needles; him talk bout a lost sheep who finally make him way home. And maybe it is afterwards, when you gather all of these crossway stories, and you put them together, that you finally see a line had been running through all of them. Sometimes you have to tell a story the way you dream a dream, and everyone know that dreams don't walk straight.

                                        Shhhhhhhhh

If I was to tell you my story crossways, I could tell it like this: Once upon a time Anansi Spider was a travelling man. Anansi travel so much that he almost got no space left in his passport for other stamps. But though he travel to Curaçao, Panama, Merica, Canada and one whole heap of other places, Anansi never yet go to England. So Anansi Spider determine in him mind that he have to reach

222

England, and sail pon the River Thames, and play cricket at Old Trafford, and say how-di-do to Mrs Queen.

Now remember Anansi was a boasy man from morning who take special care in how he dress, but he take especial care whenever him was travelling. He wouldn' show up in no nother country wearing screbbeh-screbbeh clothes. And as him was going to England, Anansi decide to really pop fashion. He get new trousers, top hat, waistcoat and even one pocket watch fi fling inside his jacket. When Anansi walk off the plane, you want to see him strutting! Eh! Anansi a lift him hat to everybody he see saying, 'Yesh mi lady, good afternoon. Yesh shir, pleasant day." (Remember, Anansi was a man with a lisp tongue.) But all the politeness what Anansi was going on with didn't stop people from looking on him funny, like they never see nothing like Anansi from the day they born. Poor Anansi was getting confuse for Anansi Spider was a famous person. Anansi name was large back home, and in Curaçao and Panama and Merica and Canada – everybody did hear bout Anansi and would run up and ask him to sign autograph whenever they sight him. Well my dears, when Anansi finally reach the Immigration desk, the gentleman behind the counter did barely have time to ask 'Business or pleasure, Sir?" when a English woman start to holler out, 'Spider! Ooooh a spider! Kill it!' And vooops! Anansi barely dodge the broom that was coming down hard on him. Voooops! Him dodge it again. Everybody now chasing after Anansi and swiping at him. Poor Anansi run and run, his eight legs moving faster than even racehorse, so fast him all tear up the new trouser pants that did specially make for him. Anansi run straight up into the ceiling and from that time till now whenever you want to find Anansi Spider you just have to look up to the ceiling because him still hiding there.

Shhhhhhhhh

If I was to tell my story crossways, I could tell it like this: Once upon a time when madness was a thing as catching as the common cold, and plenty plenty people in the world was going off their heads, a wise man decide to draw a map on his forehead. When he start walking bout with the map on his head, people at first did think that he catch the madness too. But by and by, when they realise he was still sane after all, they question him. Wise man, they ask, why you put that foolishness on your head? He gather them round and tell them. *Stop and consider something with me tonight — a man's spirit have more sense than his mind. For when we catch into a sweet worship, our spirits leave our bodies and go all bout on their own business.* Everybody nod at this for all of them had the experience of their spirits *travelling. Sometimes your spirit even travel all the way back to Africaland, or else it just roam bout for hours and sometimes for days.* Everybody nod and say yes, all of this was true. *But when it is time, those same spirits will know how to make their own way back home.* Yes, Wise Man, they tell him. You speak the truth. But aye, him finally say, *God help you if it is your mind that decide to travel! The mind have a way of getting lost. You see, it don't got no compass. It don't know left from right. It cannot give an address of where and to whom it belong. When your mind travel, plenty times it just pack up and gone for good. That is why madness is the worst affliction known unto man.* Everybody in the village see the reasoning and they all start to draw maps on their own heads and from that day on, none of them went mad again — for whenever their minds did travel, they

224

would travel with a map and could find their way home.

Shhhhhhhhh

If I was to tell my story crossways, I could tell it like this: Once upon a time Eve was in the garden dreaming bout the snake. She dream that the snake was crawling up her leg. Eve get into such a terrible fright that she jump straight out of her sleep. She look down on her leg but she never see no snake, so she say, Oh, is just dream I was dreaming, and her heart stop racing bup-di-bup-di-bup. What Eve never know is that the snake did crawl right up her leg and into her woman-parts and did find him way up inside Eve's belly. By and by she start get morning sickness, and her belly did start grow, and poor Eve frighten for she and Adam did malice each other so much over that apple business that they never did sex each other for months. So poor-mi-gal Eve don't know how she have belly. Well, nine months pass and Eve have the baby. The baby was a beautiful thing and Eve did love him so much, for she don't know that snake was the baby-daddy. And from that day on many man may seem like an archangel on the outside, but in their heart of hearts, them really is a snake.

Shhhhhhhhh

If I was to tell my story crossways, I could tell it like this: Once upon a time, long long ago, before this present God did become God, there was another God. One day this first God was bored, and did feel too coop up in Heaven where he used to stay every livelong day. He decide that he want to go out for a stroll. So God let himself out of

225

Heaven, but he go through the back door. And him walk and him walk. And him walk and him walk some more. All over the earth him walk that day, just feeling the breeze, eating guineps and dipping his two big feet into the cool river water. When evening start to come on God decide it was time to go back up to Heaven, but because the back door did lock, God had to go in the front way. Well, God come face to face with Jack Mandora. Jack Mandora was the fellow God hire to keep charge of Heaven's gate, and Jack Mandora did take his job very serious. Whole heap of people who maybe God would have did let in wasn't going to get by Jack Mandora. If your name not on the list for that day, Jack not taking out his long key and opening the gate for you. God say, *Good afternoon Jack Mandora,* and Jack Mandora say, *Good afternoon Massa God.* God say, *Jack Mandora, beg you open this gate for me so I can go back inside.* Well, what you think happen but Jack Mandora look on his list and never did see God name on it. Jack Mandora say, *bwoy, God, I woulda like to let you through you know, but I don't see your name on today's list.* God start to splutter. *But Jack, don't you see and know that Me is God?* Jack say, *Yes, Massa God, I can see that. But that don't change the fact that your name not on the list, and unless your name write down, you can't go inside.* God start get vex and say, *But this is foolishness! Why you behaving like this?* Jack Mandora stand up firm. *It is not foolishness, God, for it is you yourself who make the rules. I just following them.* Well, when God see that for true him would never get back into Heaven, he feel so sad that right there he just vanish away. That is how Jack Mandora became God in the end, and the first God turned himself into a song. Even today you will still hear people singing it.

> Keyman, keyman,
> Keyman, keyman
> Keyman lock de door and gone

> Shhhhhhhhh

If I was to tell my story crossways, I could tell it like this:
Once upon a time there was a certain chicken who could
never satisfy. Him did live in a yard and in the ground there
was plenty worms, and there was a kind farmer who did
throw plenty corn and this farmer was a man that did ongly
eat vegetables so the chicken's life was safe. But still, this
fool-fool chicken did nothing more all day than look up in
the sky and pout his lips. All his friends did warn him and
say, *you must enjoy life, Mr Chicken! You must enjoy what you have.
Plenty good things right before you and you can't even see them, for all you
do whole day is look up in the sky. All that looking up going to give you
crick-neck!* But this chicken never pay no mind. He continue
looking up to the sky, day in and day out. You could say,
his head was in the clouds. When Brother Johncrow fly by,
the chicken would moan and sigh.

> Oh me, oh my
> Poor little bud, oh my
> Look on Brother Johncrow
> *Way up high*
> Every bud but me can fly

When Brother Patoo fly by, the chicken moan and sigh
and sing the same sad song.

> Oh me, oh my
> Poor little bud, oh my

227

> Look on Brother Patoo
> *Way up high*
> *Every bud but me can fly*

And when Brother Pea Dove fly by the chicken moan and sigh and sing him song one more time.

> *Oh me, oh my*
> Poor little bud, oh my
> Look on Brother Pea Dove
> *Way up high*
> *Every bud but me can fly*

And is so him continue to sing whenever him see pigeon or hummingbird or blackbird and all the different birds that fly in the sky, until all the birds just get fed up of hearing that song. So they all get together and say, all right, chicken don't got flying feathers for true, so maybe if we each give him one of our feathers, then him can fly and he will stop moan and sigh. So all the birds give the chicken a feather. He was so glad. One by one he pluck out all of his own pretty white feathers and stick in dove feather, eagle feather, johncrow feather, hawk feather and every different kind of feather from the other birds. When him done, he did look like one big poppyshow. He don't look like no bird at all. But the chicken was proud, and he spread his wings, set to take off. But guess what happen? Chicken still couldn't fly, for it is not in the nature of chickens to reach up to the sky. And because the feathers never truly belong to him, all of them just drop right back out. So the chicken end up like that, grounded, and without a feather to call his own.

Shhhhhhhhh

And if I was to tell my story crossways, I would probably tell it like this: Once upon a time there was a leper colony in Jamaica. It was a colony for lepers but it was a beautiful place, full of every colour you can find in the rainbow. The people there did live good with each other and love was their portion, and it should have been their portion forever and ever, amen.

an instalment of a testimony spoken to the wind

Shhhhhhhh

IF I WAS to tell my story straight, the whole thing from start to finish, I would tell it like this. Hear me now and bear witness to all I say: My name is Pearline Portious, but it should have been another name. It should have been Adamine Bustamante, and that is what I call myself even today. I was born in Spanish Town, Jamaica, at 35 Queen Margaret Drive. It was a house of lepers. My mama, God bless her soul, catch her dead right there on the birthing bed and I never did know her. It was an old woman who name Agatha Lazarus who grow me instead. Mother Lazarus never did believe or mix up in the things of God, but she believe in warning. It was she who used to tell me, if fish come from river-bottom and say alligator down deh, you must believe him. Mother Lazarus dead at the grand age of 105, and it was when she gone that I finally hear the Saviour's voice. I leave everything behind me and go to live with a Warner Woman who did name Bishopess Herbert. I fall completely into Revival.

Once upon a time I was in love with a man named Lucas Gilles. I used to think that maybe this man would have did married to me. Maybe we would have made children together. Maybe in the end we would have been buried side by side in a little plot in Spanish Town. But I was a fool. I did say a terrible thing to him one night. I tell him, *Lucas, I want to leave this island because nothing is here for me.* And maybe that was what break him heart. But O, I wish

232

I wish I wish him did have the strength to say to me, *don't go, Ada. You have me. Stay with me even though I cannot promise you riches. Even though people like we will always be poor. Nothing wrong with poorness, for the Saviour say it is we who shall inherit the earth. My sweet Ada, we will live till we is old in this balmyard, and Peace and love and healing will be our portion.* But he never said none of that. Instead he help me to get to England. He help me to come to this place where I have been made to till a hard ground. It was him who write all the letters to Milton Dehaney, a man who used to be with the band once upon a time, until he migrate.

Me and this man Milton get married in England and I live with him for three years. They was three terrible years. I feel the back of Milton's hand more time than I can even count. But he never sex me in all that time. It was like his hand was firmer and stronger than his man-parts, and I get to understand that his man-parts never did work proper from morning. Maybe that is why he beat me. But I tell you what – I never hate him sake of the beating. I hate him because he was a man who did forgot all bout where he come from. He did forgot that he was a man who was revived. And him wanted me to forgot it as well. Milton find himself in a strange land and he think he could no longer sing the Lord's song here. And in the end maybe he was right, but to me life with him was like living in the Gobi desert. Most Sundays we don't even go to church. The few times that we do go he don't want to go to any jump-up church. He take me instead to a place where the service dead like dry grass that the sun burn up in June. It take me years, but finally I say enough! And on that day a powerful warning did come upon me. I wrap red and white unto my head and I put the voice of God into my mouth. I leave that yard, and I never know I was leaving it forever. When the policeman hold me that day and lock me up, Milton come with him bright self and tell the judge that I did mad from morning and he don't know what to do with me at all at all. So they fling me in the madhouse. Simple, simple like that.

When you is in a madhouse you see all manner of things, and your eyes hurt you from the visions that is not visions at all. It is all truth. Sometimes if the warden decide you is behaving too badly, he take off all your clothes and throw you into a room. The walls of this room is soft but there is really nothing soft bout it. We did call it the Pads. When warden lock the door not a stitch of light get in, and terrible things would happen inside. I tell you, if you never did mad before, you come out mad mad mad, white froth terrorising your mouth corners. And some people who was mad already, their mind torment them even worse than before, drive them even madder when they was inside that room. Some people come out and act like nothing at all was wrong, but when mealtime come is then they take the dinner knife and put it inside their necks – simple so – kill them own self, the blood spraying on to other people's food. When you inside that room and you hear the door open, sometimes you don't know if warden was coming to let you out or if Satan was letting himself in. Satan, let me tell you, was just a regular man. He did have a regular name and he did have a regular job. He did grow flowers. But he was Satan all the same because he do things to you that you spend your whole life trying to forget. When you in that room sometimes all you could do was put your hands by your arse and shit into it and maybe then you have something to protect yourself with. Perhaps you don't want to hear none of this but I talking it all the same. I talking what I don't ever talk before. Everything you ever wanted was always on the outside of that room – your clothes, your bed, your dignity. And I find out then that a man with a key is a man with a terrible power.

But what I want to say now is that I remember everything. I remember when it was that I did go looking for you, Mr Writer Man. That morning I did wake up vex and empty all at once. I say I not eating no breakfast. The nurses try to force me but I was having none of it. I take the oats and fling it clean cross the room. I take an egg and mash it in a nurse uniform. They say to me, *Pearline, we'll have to take you to Matron!* They think that would make me fraid. But I say to them, *Take me! Take me now, cause I have some questions I need to put to that miss. You think I fraid of Matron this morning? Take me now!* I bawl and scream and carry on bad, and so they drag me into Matron office. Matron did look at me and frown. *What is the problem today, Mrs Portious-Dehaney?* It was one of them days that I feel to correct her, to tell her what my name really was, but I know that it was not the day to fight that fight. So I say to her, plain and simple, *Where him is please?* She say, *Excuse me, Mrs Portious-Dehaney? Talk straight.* I bawl out, *Don't tell me to talk straight, and don't talk to me like I is no idiot. I want to know what you do with my son! I want to know where him is!* The two nurse who draw me in start to laugh and even Matron look like she want to chuckle. Then one of the nurses say, *Looks like she's having an episode today, ma'am, maybe we need to sedate her?* I turn round before they could do anything and I fire one box cross the fool-fool nurse face. Pandemonium was ready to break out but I turn back to Matron and say, My son, Ma'am. *My son who born 18 March 1976. My son who born right here in this hellhole.* Matron face turn white and she start to stammer and the fool-fool nurse who was rubbing off her face from the slap that I give her was still going on bout *sedate the mad bitch, let me inject her, Matron.* But Matron not paying them no mind any more. She sit down hard in her chair and she look at me like she ongly just see me for the first time. *Leave us for a moment,* she say to the nurses. They look at her like this time is she mad. Matron raise her voice, *I said get out!* and the two of them stumble out of the office like fraid puss. Matron look at me now and say, *Pearline, tell me, how have you remembered this all of a sudden?* I feel my knees get weak and I sit down. *All on a sudden, ma'am? All on a sudden?* I was crying now, for all the vexation gone and leave me with just emptiness. *How I could ever forget a child I give birth to, Matron? What kind of mother would I be to forget something like that?* Matron shake her head. *But that was almost five years ago, Pearline.* I never care what she say though. I tell her, Ma'am. *I can't forget him, and I want to see him now.* She say, *I don't think that is possible . . .* So I stand up and hit the desk hard and I tell her as firm as I can manage without my voice breaking, *I want to see my son!* Matron say, *Shhhhh. Shhhhh. Pearline, calm down, my dear. Calm down. I will . . . I will see what I can do. I promise you.*

I don't know how long it did take. Maybe it was the next day. Maybe it was the next year. I was sleeping in my bed and then Matron herself was pushing me awake. *Pearline, get up now. You're coming with me.* I had to rub the sleep out my eye to see that is not dream I was dreaming, but there was Matron and she not dressed in her whites as usual. She was in normal-people clothes and holding up another set of clothes which must be for me. *Come, Pearline. We don't have much time. We have to get the train.* When I finish wash my face and put on everything, she take my hand soft soft in her own and nod. *I'm so proud of you,* she say to me. *Remembering your son is a big sign of healing. You may be all right after all.* I was surprised. *You taking me to him?* I ask. *Yes, my dear. You'll get a chance to see him. We can't stay for long, though, but we'll see how this first visit goes.* Matron keep on talking, and I keep on nodding, but I did stop hearing anything she was saying. I don't believe I am going to finally see my boy. I know that it was years ago that him born, but I can't tell if it was five or fifteen. I know he was born on a day that I did open my eyes and see the spirit of death floating bout in that room. I had to speak unto that spirit in my own spirit language. I tell it seven and seven and seven. I tell it to leave in the name of the most holy Saviour, and it did leave.

That morning, it come to me that life is a terrible circle. I never know my mother and now my son don't know his. I want to make a good impression so I get worried bout how I was looking. I bout to stop Matron and tell her no, I cannot meet my boy in these hospital clothes. But when I look down I see that I was wearing clothes

I never did see before. The new clothes almost frighten me but then I remember it was Matron who did bring them. So I start rehearsing in my mind what I was going to say when I see this boy who is my son, this beautiful boy. I decide already that he is beautiful. I decide that I will be able to pick him out of a room of a thousand people, because he will be the most beautifulest of them all. I was quiet, quiet while I was walking with Matron, sitting with her on the train, walking up this road and that. I was keeping my own counsel. I ongly look up when I begin to hear schoolchildren playing. My heart like it was set to gallop right out of my chest. Matron still walking ahead, fifty yards, a hundred yards before she realise that I stop. I stop because now I see him.

My dear. I saw you. I know it was you because you was the most beautifulest boy. You was standing there in the playground and if there was a million more children I still would have known you different from the rest. I did feel so stunned I could not move my foot. It was stiff like concrete, like I was just a statue out there on the pavement, considering the words of Jesus. I watch you, how you was all by yourself. I think you was no more than six. Your skin was as pale as milk. All the other pickney them was sliding down slides, romping in the sand and kicking up dust, them was swinging on the swings and bouncing up and down on the seesaws. But there was you, just standing in the middle of it all. And maybe you decide to play make-believe. Maybe you decide to pretend to be a plane or something. For you did throw your arms wide, and you started to go Zooooooom. Zooooooom. Zooooooooom. You was spinning and spinning and zooming and spinning, so fast like you was in your own world. Then your two fists open, and your fingers was like stars, and you was holding the lower part of your belly like a woman will hold herself when she catch up in the middle of birth pain, and all the time you was still spinning. And I know what was happening to you, my child. It was the spirit. The spirit did hold you. Matron was holding me too, holding me tight around my waist and saying, *Calm down now, Pearline, Calm down! Have some control, woman!* A teacher woman walk up to you the same time looking stern and trying to tell you something as well. I think maybe she was telling you to calm down too. But the two of us wasn't paying them an earthly mind. We was Warners together. The two of us spinning that morning. The two of us shouting like Jeremiah. For the word zoooom did fall clean from your mouth and instead you was shouting the same as me, *Flood and Earthquake! Wind and Storm! Warrant!*

The End of the Story

At the end, I walk out to find Adamine once again on the balcony. The night is cold and the trees, without their leaves, are shivering. The city is spread out, twinkling like some enormous galaxy before us. I know she comes out here every night, steps softly, as if trying not to wake me. From my room I have heard her mumbling on and on, until eventually I fall asleep. There was one night, however, when I parted the curtains to see her, but then I promised myself never to do it again. I was too afraid of what I saw. It seems that my mother had adopted the habit of climbing over the railing and standing there balanced on the thin ledge, her face turned towards the city. I had to admit, her body seemed so relaxed, so unencumbered, as if she were no longer penned in by any man, or any country, or even by my story.

She spread her arms wide and said softly to the city below, 'shhhhhh' as if to hush it so it would listen to her.

But if I had witnessed her do this too often, I would have worried. I would have worried that one night she might simply step out into the night. That she would fall and fade. I could imagine her leaning forward. Slowly. Slowly. And then the air would grab her. The wind would lash her body. The ground would become something like the long arms of God and those arms would be stretched towards her.

This God would say a benediction.

'Your life was not an easy one, and now your bones are weary,

241

and you are coming to take your rest. But know this, Adamine, we have loved you.'

She would open her eyes at last to see what was coming towards her, the end of the future, the ground, her saviour's arms. But before the Warner Woman's teeth could break against the pavement, she would say unto it, 'Behold.'

And if I saw her out there on the ledge, I would worry because I know that she had tried to kill herself before. It was twenty-five years ago. She had been taken out of St Osmund's Hospital for a kind of excursion. Apparently she was being taken to meet a son she had finally remembered. It was to be the first time I would catch a glimpse of my mother.

But something happened.

Of this meeting the records simply say, 'there was a rather unfortunate and dare I say, somewhat unexplainable incident.' The report is initialled SL. Sylvia Lightbourne.

Adamine was taken back to the hospital where there seems to have been screaming and scraping and biting and scratching. There may also have been the smashing of things. She had to be tranquillised and sent to bed.

But in the night Adamine woke up. The sedatives had worn off, and without making any fuss, she wrote herself a suicide note – a simple, elegant declaration of who she was. Or perhaps it was a suggestion of what was to be put on her gravestone. *My name is Adamine Bustamante and I did born amongst the lepers.*

She took off her nightgown and the moon shone on her breasts. She ripped the nightgown in two, and tied one end around her neck. She climbed on the bed then, and had it not been for another patient who woke up just at this moment, who looked at Adamine and began to cry and to babble and to beat her chest, such a commotion which sent the night nurse running in, Adamine might have been found the next morning hanging by her nightgown. The room would have smelt of her faeces because the hanged always do this, as if in death the body tries to empty itself.

I cannot help but think these thoughts when I come to find Adamine on the balcony, on the other side of the railing, her back to me, her face towards the city. It seems, however, that she knows I am here, because she begins to speak clearly, and she is addressing me.

'My dear. I saw you. I know it was you because you was the most beautifulest boy. You was standing there in the playground and if there was a million more children I still would have known you different from the rest ...'

After she has told me all that she remembers, she asks, 'Why you never tell me from the beginning? Why you never tell me who you , and furthermore why you never tell me what you was?'

Because I wanted you to remember by yourself,' I tell her.

But you could have did tell me,' she insists. Her voice is embling. 'I did always feel so alone in this world.'

I walk up to her then and reach my arms around and I hold my mother softly. I whisper into her back.

'The Warner People is still here, Mama. We is still here. Seers. rophets. Forecasters of Earthquakes. We is here. But things is different now. We take the pencils down from behind our ears and now we is writing. We been writing one whole heap of books. And guess what, Mama? There is people who go into bookshops and they buy the things we write, and they put them on their shelves. And plenty times they don't know that all of these things they been reading was not no novel, was not no poem, was not no history book. It was a simple warning. Mama, plenty people in this world have ears but they don't know how to hear. And plenty of them have eyes, but they don't know how to see.'

✿

Eventually I go back in to finish this thing that I have been writing, and it comes to me that every book is a miracle – at once fully

243

itself, but also a portion of itself. That is to say, every book runs cover to cover, but the story within breathes its own breath, inhabits a space larger than its covers can provide. In the end every story is edited, brought down to some essence, because here is the sad truth: books end, and pages thin, and every word is pulling us towards that last, climactic full stop.

In its final moments it may feel as if the book is holding you open. It may feel as if the book's arms are spread wide, as if to embrace whoever has been holding it. Or maybe the book would simply like to say something, to look its reader in the eye, and then look just beyond.

And the book will say, Do you see what is coming towards y
Can you see over your shoulders? Warrant, the book always d

Thanks

Despite what Mr Writer Man claims in this novel, some books really start with the first sentence, and from there an entire world is born. So thanks to the unlikely progenitors of this story, Stephen es and Timothy Bingham, who were chatting away randomly night and told me a small bit of trivia – that once upon a time ere was a leper colony in Jamaica.

I will never say it enough but, again and always, to Ronald, for ur patient ears on which I have tried out so many versions of y writing. And to so many other friends who may not have own that they were being helpful when they were: Carolyn Allen ho drove me to the library in Jamaica; Christine Ferguson whose oor I've loved to knock on in Glasgow; John Guliak who heaved my writing desk and dining table and life into the new house (yes, Chapter 3 is for you!); Annie Paul who lent me that old journal on Revival with the beautiful picture of Kapo; Michael Bucknor and Tanya Shirley for being wonderful friends (you guys are the best); and Richard and Natalie and 'Optimus'(how deeply I love you guys!).

Thanks to Kirsty, my editor, who gave great advice but was also happy to trust my own ear at times and had no problems with me keeping such strange expressions as 'all on a sudden' – little things that felt right to the place and to the people I was writing about.

And to Alice, my agent, who seems always to believe me even when I'm lying and I say, *yes, yes; I really am writing; the novel is going well*. Perhaps she knows that if I lie enough it will eventually become true.

Finally, to my big sister and one of my best friends, Shauna, who believed in this long before it was written. To my father, whom I love more than I can ever tell him properly, who acted as my research assistant and told me to call Bishop Guthrie who in turn sent me to the balmyard in Watt Town where I watched Revival.

Thanks to my mother, Vivette Miller (1947–2009). It is such a terrible thing to have lost you, but I hope, one day, to find you again.